First Mate Tate

Virginia Masterman-Smith

MARSHALL CAVENDISH • NEW YORK

Text copyright © 2000 by Virginia Masterman-Smith.
Marshall Cavendish, 99 White Plains Road, Tarrytown, NY 10591

Library of Congress Cataloging-in-Publication Data
Masterman-Smith, Virginia.
First Mate Tate / by Virginia Masterman-Smith.
    p.   cm.
Summary: Her parents' gambling addiction robs twelve-year-old First Mate
of her childhood as she must care for her younger siblings and earn money
to pay family expenses.
ISBN 0-7614-5075-0
[1. Family problems—Fiction. 2. Child abuse—Fiction. 3. Gambling—Fiction.
4. Moneymaking projects—Fiction.] I. Title.
PZ7.M42387 Fi 2000   [Fic]—dc21   00-035867

First Edition
Book design by Constance Ftera
Printed in the United States of America

*This book is dedicated to my sisters,
Doris and Michele.*

1

Daddy dangled Elizabeth out the window. He had her by the ankles. She laughed so hard. She thought it a big joke.

"Everything looks so little on the ground!"

Mom didn't think it was funny.

"Stop it! Stop it!"

She stood behind Daddy wringing her hands. She was very good at hand wringing.

"Only when you tell me where you hid my money," he said.

He meant the grocery money. Mom didn't have a clue where it was because First Mate had hidden it.

First Mate was the eldest kid in the Tate family, twelve going on forty. She was in Gram's old room fixing the awful coat she wore when she made her Tate Bank collections. That's what she called her loan business . . . Tate Bank. Daddy didn't know about it, or he wouldn't have wasted time hanging Elizabeth out the window.

He had the itch again. That's what Grams had always called his gambling crazies.

The other Tate kids, Barry, Ferdy, Christopher, and PJ

jumped up and down on Elizabeth's bed, sing-songing at the top of their lungs:

"Drop her, Daddy, drop.
Drop her, Daddy, drop.
Drop her, Daddy.
Drop her, Daddy.
Drop her, Daddy drop."

(Except Christopher didn't sing. He stuttered too much.)

PJ sprang high enough to touch the ceiling. He was ten.

"Get First Mate!" Mom hollered at him.

She screamed three more times before PJ bounced off the bed and ran to Grams's old room. Grams was dead, so the room was the catch-all.

PJ didn't bother to try the door because First Mate always locked it. Instead, he pounded with both fists.

"First Mate, Mommy wants you."

First Mate glared at the door. When she got mad, her eyes went on fire, and she was so mad she could have burnt a hole clear through to PJ. She had Daddy's eyes, gray at the moment, to match her sweat suit. Everybody said they were beautiful, but she didn't have time to care.

She was putting the day's envelopes in order. She had to sort them according to her route, which she changed every week for safety's sake. She carried a lot of money in that old coat.

"Why don't you break the door down?" she called to PJ.

"Mommy wants you."

"You told me already—so get lost!"

Mom always wanted First Mate for one thing or another.

She put the Ocean Road envelopes at the bottom of the pile. They'd be last, today. First, she'd work her way toward the cemetery. She hadn't been there since the funeral. Well, that was Grams's fault for dying. She'd promised she wouldn't, at least until the kids got brought up. First Mate put half the envelopes in one pocket and the other half in the other.

"*Better come out. Mommy wants you. She's having a fit!*" PJ roared.

"So what else is new?" First Mate called, as she checked her flashlight.

She wouldn't finish before dark. That was for sure.

PJ stopped pounding.

Relieved, First Mate hung the coat in the closet. She loved that coat. It had been Grams's . . . a shaggy memory of her trip to the Arctic. Grams had said she'd get buried in it, but she didn't, so First Mate took it before Mom could throw it away. Mom didn't care that Grams was probably the first woman to travel the Arctic Ocean in a ship that cut through ice.

PJ started on the door again.

"*First Mate, Elizabeth's crying. Daddy won't pull her in.*"

First Mate's heart did a flip.

"Why didn't you tell me?"

She ran to the door.

"You didn't ask," PJ said, as she opened it.

First Mate pushed PJ out of the way and raced to Elizabeth's room. The nearer she got the louder the hullabaloo.

"Drop her, Daddy, drop.
Drop her, Daddy, drop.
Drop her, Daddy.
Drop her, Daddy.
Drop her, Daddy drop."

First Mate barged in.

"Get off that bed, you three—and make it. You think Mom has nothing else to do but make Elizabeth's bed?"

The fact was that the beds got made only on Saturday when First Mate and Mom changed the sheets—that is, if Mom was home—but Barry, Christopher, and Ferdy knew better than to argue with their big sister. They tumbled off and grabbed Elizabeth's quilt.

"She peed the bed again," Barry shouted, but nobody paid attention.

Daddy leaned out the window. Mom pulled on his arm but not too hard, or he might drop Elizabeth, whom no one could see at the moment. Everyone heard her, though, squealing like a piglet.

"I don't want to play anymore. I'm cold."

Elizabeth stared at the high bushes two stories below. In front of them were some naked bushes, and in front of them was the grass. She had goose bumps all over.

"Let me in now, Daddy," she wailed.

It's a wonder the whole town of Shadow Lawn, New Jersey, didn't hear her. However, it was winter, and everybody's windows were shut tightly. It was also morning. Nobody was on the street, yet.

"Damn! How long has she been out there?" First Mate asked her mother.

"Where's the grocery money? Where did you hide it?" Mom whispered.

First Mate pushed past her mother to her father. She looked at the soles of Elizabeth's patent leather shoes and down at her red corduroy slacks. She was dressed up for Valentine's Day.

"Elizabeth, honey, I'm here," First Mate called.

"I'm cold," Elizabeth cried.

"Daddy, the kid's going to get pneumonia."

"Fly like a butterfly, sing like a bird," Pete Tate called, as he swung Elizabeth back and forth.

"You want to come in?" First Mate asked her sister.

"My head hurts," Elizabeth wailed. "It's like a balloon ready to pop. Tell Daddy I don't want to play anymore."

"Daddy, her head hurts!"

"It does not. She's having fun," he grinned.

A shiver ran through First Mate. Her father's eyes

glittered that crazy way . . . like the lights were on, but nobody was home.

"Please, Pete," Mom whimpered from behind him and First Mate.

First Mate turned around. Her mother was crying. Gad! Disgusting!

The boys sat on the newly made bed, four kids with front row seats at the fights. First Mate scowled at them.

"G'wan downstairs and get your coats on. It's time for the bus. And don't forget your Valentines."

It was Thursday, February 14, Valentine's Day.

"What about Elizabeth?" Barry asked.

"What about her?" First Mate blasted.

One threatening step toward him and the four boys scurried like squirrels. As soon as they were gone, First Mate told her father: "You drop my sister, and you die."

"Who's going to kill me . . . you?" he replied, sarcastically.

First Mate's stomach was as tight as her fists.

"No, the state of New Jersey. They'll put a needle in your arm, and I'll watch until every breath seeps from your body. You'll be a corpse, and I'll laugh. . . ."

Elizabeth's screams reached the desperation pitch.

"Don't you know? One little mistake, and she's gone! Nobody will say you were playing a game. People will call you a murderer."

"What makes you think that I'll drop her?" he asked.

"What makes me think you won't?"

"Because *I'm* holding her."

Mom had retreated to the bed. She sat at the edge, rocking back and forth.

"Okay, that's it. I'm calling the police," First Mate declared, heading for the door.

Mom jumped up and blocked First Mate's way.

"How embarrassing! Don't you dare."

"Wait 'til the police get here. Now that's embarrassing!" First Mate replied.

Nonetheless, she stopped. Daddy never did drop Elizabeth. There was always that fear, though.

"Never mind the smart talk, First Mate, just tell me where you hid my money," Daddy demanded.

"It isn't your money. It's *our* money . . . our *grocery* money. After you bounce my baby sister on her head, will you starve the rest of us to death?"

"Tell him, First Mate!" Mom pleaded.

"You told me not to, not under any circumstances," First Mate retorted.

"She's been out there too long. Please," Mom pleaded.

Outside the window was quiet. Elizabeth wasn't whimpering any more. Had she fainted? Was she freezing to death?

"Bring her in, and I'll tell you," First Mate promised her father.

"Forget it," he said. "Once she's in, you'll never tell me."

"Daddy, she's your baby girl," First Mate reminded him.

"So are you, and you know where my money is."

"Suppose you lose? How do you expect us to eat next week?"

"I won't lose," Daddy said. "I've got a hunch."

First Mate softened her tone. "Daddy, you had a hunch a month ago, and it didn't pan out. I had to pay the mortgage."

"I paid you back. Didn't I?" Daddy said.

Elizabeth let out a wail. First Mate sighed in relief.

"The money's in the bottom of the wood box in the living room," she told her father.

He hauled Elizabeth inside. Her face was blood red, and she was crying, but Daddy gave her a bear hug and said what a fine little girl she was and what a fun game they'd played . . . didn't they? . . . And Elizabeth grinned. Mom wrapped Elizabeth in her quilt, and hugged and kissed her. Daddy made a beeline for the door.

First Mate sat next to her mother, playing with Elizabeth's soft curls while she waited for her to get warm enough to go downstairs. The bed smelled of urine.

"You've got to do something about your husband," First Mate said.

"Shhh," Mom replied.

"He's getting worse!"

"Shhh!"

Mom nodded toward Elizabeth, cozy at last inside the quilt.

"As if she doesn't know her father's a nut," First Mate snapped.

Mom glared at her.

"Are you okay to go to school, Sweetie Pie?" she asked Elizabeth. "You don't want to miss Valentine's Day. Do you?"

Elizabeth poked her head from under the quilt. She looked okay, none the worse, really.

"Did you put your Valentines in your book bag?" First Mate asked.

Elizabeth nodded the affirmative.

"Good. Go get your coat on. I'll ride you to school in my bike basket."

Elizabeth's eyes danced. Such a prize was worth hanging all day out the window. She hugged Mom and pulled away from the quilt.

"See you later, alligator," Elizabeth grinned at First Mate.

First Mate couldn't get herself to return the usual, "In a while, crocodile." Her lips wouldn't form the words. They wouldn't loosen enough to allow even the hint of a smile. She watched Elizabeth disappear down the hall.

Mom pulled the quilt around herself.

"Close the window. It's cold," she told First Mate.

First Mate hadn't realized that the window was still open. She stared at Elizabeth's *Alice in Wonderland* curtains flapping in the winter breeze. The March Hare's hat rippled over the Tardy Rabbit.

"I thought you should know that I lied. The money isn't in the wood box," she told her mother.

2

First Mate was very late for school, which gave Elizabeth an extra special ride because First Mate gunned her old bike as if she were in the Grand Prix. She spun around corners and jumped curbs. Elizabeth hoped for a pop-a-wheelie. She didn't dare ask, not with her sister in such a snit. Elizabeth couldn't figure First Mate out. One minute she was mad; the next minute she was glad; then she was mad all over again.

The bike bounced over the bump into the schoolyard driveway. First Mate pedaled to the bike racks and braked. Elizabeth climbed out of the basket.

First Mate backed the bike into an empty slot. She couldn't fit it front-first like all the others because her enormous newspaper basket stuck out too far. One of these days she was going to get rid of her paper route, but until then she had to put up with a rear-end-first-parked bike. The thought of it caused her mood to be worse than it already was.

"Need ice cream?" she grumbled at Elizabeth, who nodded the affirmative; First Mate pressed two shiny quarters into her sister's small hand.

"Don't tell the boys."

Elizabeth nodded the negative.

"Hugs?" Elizabeth asked.

"Hugs," First Mate replied, bending down to wrap her arms around her baby sister.

"Kisses?" Elizabeth whispered into First Mate's ear.

First Mate brushed her lips lightly against the six-year-old's. She didn't realize that she'd smiled, but Elizabeth saw it and skipped triumphantly to the first-grade line. Fortunately, she didn't see the scowl return as First Mate headed for the upper-grades' entrance. The principal was afoot; Iron Nail Vail, the students called her because she ruled with an iron pen and was hard as nails.

Iron Nail was never without a pad of detention slips. They came in triplicate, a yellow copy for the office, a pink copy for the teacher, and a white copy for parents. The school mailed the parents' copy in an official envelope. To date, First Mate had collected one hundred sixty-five of them.

The parents' copy was mailed home, and since mail made Mom nervous, First Mate brought it in everyday. She always put the bills in Mom's desk in the living room. That way, Mom didn't have to look at them until First Mate brought home Daddy's paycheck on Friday afternoon.

Paychecks started last year. When Daddy owned Tate Boat Works and Marina, he didn't need one. When the business was his, the money was his; but now the business wasn't his anymore. Charlie "the Creep" Fisk owned it.

The problem was that Daddy lost more than he won at the casinos in Atlantic City. That made him nervous, so he gambled more. A year ago last Thanksgiving, Charlie took over.

PJ had an inkling of what had happened, although First Mate insisted he was all wet. On Thanksgiving morning, he and First Mate were helping their father haul in the last boats for winter storage. PJ hooked the sterns; First Mate hooked the bows. Daddy ran the rig, hoisting the boats from the river and depositing them on the scaffold. It was great fun to watch those boats sail in the air, dripping like overworked air conditioners in the middle of August.

All of a sudden, a yellow Maserati pulled into the empty parking lot. A thick-necked man in church clothes got out and swaggered up the steps to the office. Daddy turned off the crane.

"That's it, kids. No more for today. Go on home and help your mother roast the turkey."

He jumped down and raced up the office steps.

"Who's that man?" PJ asked First Mate.

"Somebody important enough to make our father run like hell," she replied.

Thanksgiving dinner was like a last meal before the execution, except First Mate couldn't decide who would go first, her father or her mother. One looked bleak; the other kept running to the kitchen to cry. The kids didn't seem to notice, except PJ, so First Mate gave him her turkey leg.

"I told you," he whispered, "something's wrong."

"I told you," she hissed back, "you're all wet!"

After breakfast the next morning, PJ and First Mate pedaled down to the marina to help their father finish with the boats. Daddy was in the office with that man, whom he introduced as Charlie.

"Charlie's our new, uh, office manager," he told them.

Charlie wore another church outfit and soft leather shoes with thin soles.

"You don't know much about marinas, do you?" First Mate remarked. Nobody hung around a dock in a tailored suit and leather shoes.

Charlie gave her father daggers for a glance. Daddy turned green. He said, "You kids go on home. I don't need you, today. Charlie and I have to work on the books."

Who was he trying to fool? The books—Mom did the books. PJ started to say so, but First Mate gave him her own version of a dagger look, so he shut up.

"Let's go to the Station and do some serious damage to a couple of hot fudge sundaes," she suggested.

"Your dollar?" PJ grinned.

"Daddy's dollar," First Mate smiled, winking at her father.

Daddy said, "Thank you" with his eyes. He used to do that. They twinkled, not a crazy twinkle, just a nice glow that made First Mate feel good. He pulled out a ten-dollar bill and handed it to her.

"Is that enough?"

"Fine," she nodded, and they left.

19

"I don't like that guy," PJ told First Mate, as they descended the steps.

"Me neither," First Mate agreed.

They reached their bikes. First Mate had a fancy one, then.

"Something's wrong . . . I think . . . maybe," PJ said. "Let's go back upstairs. Daddy might need us."

They didn't go back, but they *did* climb to the roof and look through the skylight to see what was going on in the office. If that "Charlie" fellow had a gun on their father, they'd jump through the skylight so fast he wouldn't know what hit him.

They were more than surprised to see Charlie sitting at their father's desk, going through the books. Daddy looked sick.

"I guess we watch too many police shows on TV," First Mate whispered. "Race you to the Station."

The Station was Shadow Lawn's fanciest ice cream parlor. It was part of the Pennsylvania Railroad's Shadow Lawn Station. First Mate never took her brothers and sister there, anymore. The ice cream was homemade and very expensive.

She let PJ beat her that day. She made believe her bicycle gears got stuck in neutral. She told Mom that, too, when she traded in the best bike in Shadow Lawn for the rattletrap she needed to deliver newspapers, plus three hundred dollars. She said the bike looked great but it wasn't dependable.

What a crock! Daddy was the one who wasn't dependable anymore. He'd rolled his paycheck away at the craps table in Atlantic City. Mom was crying because the house was cold. The gas company had turned off the heat, and she was too embarrassed to tell them her kids might freeze to death. After that, First Mate collected Daddy's paychecks.

Now, she collected detention slips. She'd wanted to tack them onto the walls of the new room Daddy'd built for her upstairs in the attic, but Mom would have a fit if she saw them.

Once, Daddy nearly mugged First Mate for his paycheck . . . chased her down the office steps. She was so scared she jumped them all.

She was up and over the fence to the yacht club before she knew she'd climbed it. Daddy was right behind her, so she squirreled herself out through a hole under the fence on the other side and ran until she couldn't breathe anymore.

That night she hid in the woods near the cemetery. By the time she got the nerve to go home, her father had already left for Atlantic City. That was the night he pawned Grams's good silver. First Mate wondered how much he got for it.

One hundred sixty-six detention slips pilfered from the mailbox were no big deal. First Mate's major offense was homework. She never did it. By February of her second year in eighth grade, most of the teachers didn't bother to write her up. A few still did on principle. That made up one hundred forty-nine detentions. One detention was for calling Mrs. Quirk, her homeroom teacher, a —. Sixteen more were for tardiness. They weren't her fault, so why should she have to pay?

First Mate had tried many times to explain this to Iron Nail in a very roundabout manner, of course. However, Iron Nail wasn't good at reading between the lines, so First Mate declared she was "too busy for such frivolity as detention." Iron Nail didn't agree and that was unfortunate because First Mate didn't need another enemy.

Iron Nail waited at the end of the hall. Gritting her teeth, First Mate approached.

"Morning, Miss Vail," First Mate said.

"Morning, Miss Vail," she heard behind her. The nutra-sweet voice belonged to the one-and-only, only one—Jessica McLean—as in strawberry-blond curly hair and Neiman-Marcus outfits.

Just before school began last September, Jessica and family moved into a ritzy townhouse in a complex called Ocean's Edge. Jessica's father drove a Ferrari and her mother a Jaguar four-door sedan. Jessica walked on water, or so she thought, and most of the kids in the eighth grade at Ferris Antoon School believed it enough to elect her class vice-president.

First Mate had campaigned against her, on the grounds that Jessica "hadn't paid her dues," which meant that as a new kid in Shadow Lawn, she had no right to do anything but be nice.

"She *is* nice," Tommy Callahan told First Mate. Billy Beak was already in love with Jessica, so he said, "Stuff it."

Then Jessica told Billy that First Mate was trash.

"Look at the way she dresses. It's embarrassing!"

Billy agreed. First Mate dressed like a tar . . . deck shoes, sailor hat, sweats.

"That's because I'll own my father's marina someday," First Mate told him. "What's Neiman-Marcus going to own after she pays my bill?"

Jessica already owed First Mate a mint. They decided to call a truce; Jessica needed First Mate; First Mate needed her business. However, that did not mean they were friends!

Like First Mate, Jessica wasn't in the best of moods when she arrived at school that morning. In fact, a similar riot at *her* home had caused her to be late. At a time of such distress, the one person she did not need standing ahead of her was Miss First Mate Tate!

Jessica pushed ahead and handed Miss Vail a perfumed note.

"Duh, I believe I was first," First Mate said.

The note smelled of icky lavender. First Mate held her nose. Jessica caught the action from the corner of her eye and stepped back, crunching First Mate's toe with her thick, stylish heel.

"No problem. It's just a toe. I have nine others," First Mate muttered, but that wasn't a good enough retaliation. "And what does Mummy have to tell Missy Vail?" she whispered into Jessica's ear.

If Miss Vail heard, she didn't let on.

"You still have detention, my dear," she told Jessica, returning the perfumed note.

"Oh yes, of course, Ma'am. I'll be there," Jessica replied, backing up.

Crunch! First Mate now suffered two lobsters in the steam pot. Another toe fell to the massive heel of Miss Jessica McLean.

"So sorry," Jessica said, her voice oozing sarcasm.

"Fear not. Time heals all and time wounds all heels," First Mate replied, blandly.

Good retort, she thought.

Miss Vail motioned Jessica toward the lockers. She and First Mate watched her saunter down the hall. As soon as Jessica was out of earshot, Miss Vail asked.

"And what's your excuse, Emily?"

First Mate's face turned as red as her two toes. No one but Grams ever called her Emily. Emily was a family secret. The name was on her birth and baptismal certificates, but that was all. Cappy Tate, her grandfather, had dubbed her First Mate at the baptism party.

The whole family plus a hundred or so of everybody's best friends were sailing down the Navasink River in the *Mayflower*, which was Cappy's yacht. Emily, not yet First Mate, was three months old and didn't have any sea legs. She cried up a storm. Mom changed her, fed her, and patted her for burps. Grams rocked her. Daddy cuddled her. Just about every one of the hundred or so guests tried to get the baby to stop yowling.

Finally, Cappy put the baby on his shoulder and carried her up to the pilothouse. Actually, he was uncomfortable having someone else in charge of his boat, but Grams had insisted because she wanted Cappy at the party with the family.

Cappy took a seat next to the captain, a very seaworthy buddy from their days in the Navy. Baby Emily opened her eyes and looked around. Then she reached for the wheel. Of course, she couldn't hold it. She couldn't hold anything yet. She was too young.

"Look at that. She wants to pilot. Did you ever see such a thing? She's a boss and born for the sea," Cappy said. "I ought to name her after me, but there's only one Cappy in this world, so she'll have to be my First Mate."

When he rejoined the party, the baby was asleep in his arms.

"From here on in, we call this child First Mate. No Emily! A name that pale couldn't weather a thunder-storm, nevermind a full-blown nor'easter."

"You can't name her. She's not your baby," Grams told Cappy.

She was the only person in the world with the nerve to buck him.

Cappy gave his son, First Mate's father, a look to wither a whale.

"What is it, pale Emily or powerful First Mate?"

Daddy shrugged. He looked at Mom. She shrugged.

"First Mate's as good a nickname as any," he told Cappy.

"Heaven help us," Grams sighed.

"Her name is First Mate," Cappy declared.

From that day on, everyone except Grams called Emily, First Mate. Mom and Daddy actually began to like it. They said the name was . . . uh . . . different.

When the rest of the Tate kids were born, Mom and Daddy made sure they picked names Cappy liked. PJ was Peter III, after his father, grandfather, and Peter the Great, who started the Russian Navy. Barry was named for Commodore Barry, the founder of the United States Navy. Christopher was named for Christopher Columbus, and everybody knows what he did. Ferdy was for Ferdinand Magellan, the first to sail around the tip of Africa and reach the East. Elizabeth's name came from the great Queen Elizabeth I of England. She'd founded the *English* Navy.

Miss Vail didn't like being told that detention was a waste of First Mate's time. She also was furious that the kid cut daily. Consequently, she typed off a memo to First Mate's teachers.

"Please call First Mate Tate by her legal name, Emily. First Mate is not a name. It is a title."

Mrs. Quirk replied, "Been there—done that—please note detention slip for October 22. The dear child called me—"

Mr. Harley repled, "Suggest you write off monster as

loss to the community. Don't waste time with Emily, First Mate, or whatever she decides to call herself. Too many nice kids to worry about in this school."

Iron Nail Vail caved in to her staff. However, when she and First Mate were alone, First Mate was Emily, which was the case the morning after First Mate's father hung Elizabeth out the second-floor window.

"What is the excuse, Emily?" Iron Nail repeated, relishing every inch of embarrassment on First Mate's face.

"My baby alligator ate the alarm clock," she replied.

Miss Vail didn't raise an eyebrow. "Mmm, that's detention seventeen for tardiness."

"Is it a record?" First Mate asked.

"Counting the hundred forty-nine you owe for home-work, plus one for —." "I paid for that. I went to detention," First Mate cut in.

Miss Vail ignored her. "I suppose it is a record of a sort, Emily," she said. "Would you please tell me why you bother to take books home?"

"It makes my parents feel good," First Mate shrugged.

Miss Vail pointed to the lockers, and First Mate took off. Jessica was just locking up when she arrived.

"Step on my toe again and I'll call your two hundred thirty-five dollar note," First Mate warned her.

She should have done that when she had the chance.

3

For ten percent interest a week, a reliable kid could borrow up to three hundred dollars from Tate Bank. "Reliable" meant the client could keep his or her mouth shut and had the wherewithal to keep up the weekly payments. That is, ten percent interest plus ten percent of the principle of the loan. Jessica was an excellent client.

"I honestly am sorry about your toe. I forgot you were behind me," she oozed, as she put away her locker key.

First Mate had just opened her locker.

"Did you think I'd evaporated?" she asked.

"No, I forgot about you," Jessica said.

"Well, don't forget to keep your feet to yourself."

It was a terrible retaliation to Jessica's excellent diss. First Mate was so annoyed with herself that she slammed her locker door hard enough to bring three teachers to their classroom doorways. First Mate pointed to Jessica.

"She's having a bad hair day."

Blood rose in Jessica's face. By the time she reached the teachers' doorways, she was purple, a sure sign of guilt. First Mate gloated.

"Yes! There is a God—maybe."

It seemed to her that God had died along with Grams,

for it was after her funeral that First Mate's world took a nosedive . . . or maybe a belly flop. Either way, it brought her a sour stomach and a big headache.

Grams had always been able to keep Daddy away from the casinos, or at least made his trips to Atlantic City more miserable than staying home. Her formula was simple. Daddy's eyes always gave him away. There was a glint in them whenever he got the "itch."

When Grams saw the glint, she followed Daddy around like a puppy's tail. She went with him to the boat yard; she stayed with him in the office, she sat near any boat he worked on in the shop. Grams even guarded the bathroom when he was in it. There was no way First Mate's father could sneak off to the big AC (Atlantic City) without Grams.

A couple of times, Daddy took Grams with him. She hollered and nagged the entire two hours down the Garden State Parkway. At the casino, any casino, it didn't matter, Grams followed Daddy from one craps table to another, wailing about how her son gambled the food from his babies' mouths.

"Six babies! Six little babies home with their mother," she'd tell everyone.

Craps is a game that needs focus. Neither Daddy nor any of the gamblers could think. The casino was losing money. They paid Daddy to take his mother home.

Just before she died, Grams gave Mom the formula. Unfortunately, First Mate's mother was not her grandmother. Mom tried. She drove regularly with Daddy to Atlantic City, but she didn't have the gift.

Mom bombed nagging and flopped whining. She was a total turkey in the hollering department. She didn't know how to holler. She screeched sometimes, but she just couldn't get up a good holler.

First Mate was more like Grams had been. She could holler anybody down, even Daddy at home, but he never took her to Atlantic City. She was too young to gamble.

So First Mate turned to God. She prayed and prayed and prayed some more. She went to church with the family on Sundays and sang hymns louder than anybody in the congregation. She put an angel on the kitchen windowsill. She lit a candle in front of the Madonna on Grams's dresser every night.

To be certain God knew she meant business, First Mate let her brothers and sister play in Noah's Ark. That was her treehouse. It was a houseboat that Grampa Cappy built with his own hands. He built it in the boat yard, towed it home, and hired a derrick to set it in the tallest tree in the Tate back yard. Cappy built three more treehouses before he died, but none as big, none as beautiful, and none as high in the sky as First Mate's Noah's Ark.

"Please make my father stop gambling," First Mate begged God.

Daddy got worse, Mom got whinier, and First Mate got mad. She quit church in favor of a Sunday paper route. Then she got the daily paper route. No time for church; no time for angels; no time for lighting candles; no time for God.

Of course having the best and only paper route in Shadow Lawn was an answer to a prayer, sort of. It put dinner on the table when Daddy gambled away the grocery money. It paid for a lot of other things, too, like the mortgage last month. Luckily, her father won for a change and paid First Mate back. In a bad month, that paper route account dropped to a fearfully low amount.

Mom deposited First Mate's newspaper earnings in a cosigned account at First Bank of Shadow Lawn. Cosigned meant Mom could take money from it any time she pleased, but First Mate couldn't because she was only twelve. For First Mate to withdraw her own money from her own account, she had to have her mother cosign.

Tad Robertson was the reason for the rule. He was forever working on some lunatic project that cost more money than his allowance allowed.

Tad's father was a big shot at First Bank, so Tad had all sorts of money in all sorts of accounts there. He would have taken out every penny, except Mr. Robertson put the kibosh on his and *every other kid's* account. First Mate hated Tad for that.

On the other hand, Tad was the reason First Mate would some day buy back Tate Boat Works and Marina. It was Tad who'd given her the idea to open Tate Bank. Last year, when First Mate was in eighth grade and Tad was only in seventh, they were walking home from school.

Actually, it was Angel Wilson, Billy Beak, Tad Robertson, and First Mate Tate walking home from school. They all lived in the same neighborhood. Tad, Billy, and First Mate were born there. Angel moved next door to Billy a year before Grams died. She and Billy were best of friends until Billy lost his mind over Jessica McLean. Now, Billy didn't have time for Angel. Besides, Jessica was jealous of her, so Billy kept his distance. That left room for First Mate. She and First Mate were new best friends.

Tad was everybody's best friend, Billy, Angel, and First Mate. However, he was truly in love with whatever scientific or non-scientific invention he was working on at the time. At that time, Tad was inventing an aerocar. That is, a car that drives and flies. He got the idea when the basketball team got stuck in traffic one day and had to forfeit a game.

Tad was a genius. He'd already put much of the thing together, and nobody doubted he'd finally work out all the kinks. The problem was his father. Mr. Robertson didn't give a hoot about inventions. The only reason he fixed over the old barn for Tad to work in was to keep him from destroying the house. Tad had a knack for accidents. Once, he almost blew up the place.

The aerocar was Tad's biggest project to date, and it cost him a fortune. The afternoon he, First Mate, Angel, and Billy walked home from school, Tad was groaning and moaning about money.

First Mate burst out laughing. "Your father owns the bank!"

"And that's where he keeps his money," Tad griped.

". . . puts me on an allowance. How am I supposed to invent a car that flies on an allowance? Have you any idea how much parts cost—even in a junkyard?"

First Mate didn't. Neither did Angel or Billy, so Tad raved on and on about his expenses until First Mate got so tired of listening to him that she offered to lend him some money.

"With interest, of course," she said.

"How much interest?" he asked.

First Mate knew from papers in the living room desk that her parents paid twenty-five percent a week on a loan they got from someone in Atlantic City. That was another hush-hush she wasn't supposed to know. The name on the loan wasn't Charles Fisk, but First Mate knew that loan sharks have aliases.

"Ten percent a week. I lend you ten dollars. You pay me a dollar interest. You pay a dollar on the loan, too. The next week, you only owe nine dollars, so you pay ninety cents interest and ninety cents on the loan which is also called the principal. And so on and so on," First Mate said, generously.

She was being kind. In another act of compassion, she decided that if Tad couldn't pay his bill on any given week, she wouldn't add the money he should have paid to the money he still owed.

Charlie was not at all good-hearted. When her mother and father couldn't pay, the interest as well as the principal was added to their loan. They'd borrowed $10,000. The first week, they had to pay back $2500 interest and $2500 on the loan. When the loan was down to $4000, they missed a payment . . . $1000 for interest and $1000 for the loan. The $2000 they missed was added to the $4000, so the loan went up to $6000! That Charlie was pure slime!

"If you can't pay one week, I won't add the principal to the loan," she told Tad. "But I'll add the interest."

"Which means?" Tad asked.

"Which means, if you don't pay two dollars back the first week, I'll just add one dollar to your actual loan, which means that you'll owe me eleven dollars instead of ten dollars.

Billy and Angel were impressed.

"How'd you dream that up so fast?" Billy asked.

"I'm brilliant." First Mate told him.

"My father's bank charges 10 percent a year interest, and he never adds interest to principal," Tad said.

"So borrow money from your father's bank," First Mate shrugged.

"Stinks," Tad said.

Everybody laughed.

That night Tad was on the phone.

"You really mean it?" he asked First Mate.

"Mean what?" First Mate snapped.

She was in another snit. Mom had stuck her with the kids again, while she drove down with Daddy to the big AC. Mom said if she didn't stick to him like glue, he'd gamble the house away.

That was a lie. The house was not in Daddy's name. Mom had talked him into deeding it over to her—but First Mate didn't know that.

"You'll lend me the money I need," Tad said.

"How much do you need?" First Mate asked.

"Fifty dollars. . . ."

When it came to numbers, First Mate's mind worked faster than Albert Einstein on a calculator. Five dollars interest the first week; four dollars and fifty cents the next—nearly $50 she'd earn fair and square for lending Tad $50! It was beautiful—clean—no fuss . . . no muss . . . just lend him $50! First Mate had to deliver a lot of newspapers to earn that much!

"Do you know what you're getting yourself into?" she asked Tad.

"Yeah, I'm getting myself the ball bearings I need for the wings," Tad told her.

"You're paying me $50 to borrow $50," First Mate told Tad.

"Yeah, but it's not all at once. Don't worry. I can pay you back. Fifty dollars is chicken feed."

That was the beginning of Tate Bank. Word about it popped around the school like corn in the microwave. Kids were begging, pleading with First Mate to lend them money. How could she refuse?

First Mate used Tad's money to buy herself a professional ledger and a box of envelopes. She took bunches of money wrappers from the marina office. She already had loads of rubber bands to wrap the newspapers. She didn't lend big money, not at first, not until she learned which kids she could trust.

The next marking period, she failed math. In fact, she failed everything, she was so busy building up her bank. So who cared, anyway?

First Mate signed her report card and handed it in. On graduation day, Daddy got the itch, and he and Mom drove down to Atlantic City. He won, and gave First Mate $500 for graduation.

"I told you I'd make it up to you, Baby, for not being there for your graduation."

He didn't even know she got left back.

It was Mom who first found out that First Mate didn't graduate. She bumped into Miss Vail at the supermarket. One word borrowed two, and two words borrowed "oh-oh," and Mom flew home like a rabid ferret.

"I don't want to go to high school," First Mate told her parents. I'm only twelve. Everybody else in the class is fourteen. I'm too young."

"But you're so smart," Mom said.

"What's so smart about letting those teachers skip me to higher grades all the time?" First Mate asked.

"You only skipped twice," Daddy said.

"So now I'll have to even things up and be left back twice," First Mate said.

That set off a major riot in which Daddy almost threw PJ's stool through the kitchen window. Actually, he wanted to throw First Mate, but Mom told him to take the stool.

First Mate shooed the kids outside.

"You want me to go to summer school. Fine—I'll give up my paper route," she told her parents.

"Which means?" Daddy asked.

"Which means you'll have to give up Atlantic City."

Needless to say, First Mate did not go to summer school. Instead, she threw the kids out of Noah's Ark and spent the summer installing Tate Bank Headquarters there. She had Tad connect it with electricity. What a genius! He tied her into the house fuse box and buried the line all the way to the tree. The electricians had just finished connecting Tad's barn, so he knew just what to do. He even knew how to install outlets for plugs!

That cost First Mate a pretty penny. In the end, Tad didn't owe Tate Bank. Tate Bank owed him.

"Keep it in my account—ten percent interest a week," Tad told First Mate.

She kept the money until he installed padlocks on the portal. Then she returned it, with interest.

"Tate Bank has closed its deposit department," she told him, which wasn't very bright because when she needed help rigging booby traps on the steps, Tad wasn't interested.

She figured out her own traps, paint cans from the marina and manure from Angel's horses, Sasha and Pasha. Angel was only too glad to be rid of it, especially in the summer.

First Mate dragged an old door from the cellar and turned it into a desk. She turned her toy chest into a vault. She glued tarpaper to the portholes and stole some old ship's lamps from the boat works. Last of all, she bought a mini 'fridge and a hot plate at the second-hand store. She plugged them in and made some iced tea. Angel brought homemade cookies, and the two celebrated the opening of Tate Bank. Billy and Tad were at a Yankees game that day.

In September, First Mate returned to Ferris Antoon School. She wasn't yet thirteen years old, but she wasn't too much younger than Angel, Billy, and Tad.

4

Billy Beak's trouble started the minute he caught sight of Miss Jessica McLean. He saw that strawberry blond hair and fell hook, line, and sinker. Billy had red hair, too, but until then he'd never really had a *girlfriend*. Angel Wilson was the closest to that, but she was really just a buddy.

Jessica was a whole new act. First Mate and Angel had to admit Jessica was beautiful. Jessica had a figure to die for. Jessica walked like a model. Jessica's smile was a billboard advertisement for toothpaste. Jessica talked like a bottle of olive oil.

Billy, the most regular kid heaven ever put on this earth, became a bloomin' fool. For Valentine's Day, he borrowed a fortune that he couldn't afford.

First Mate should have turned him down, but when he promised that if he couldn't keep up the payments, he'd give her his new bike, she doled out the money. The bike was without a doubt the most gorgeous in the bikeracks. It was even nicer than the one First Mate sold for three hundred dollars! She drooled over it daily.

That Valentine's Day morning, when Jessica arrived late to English class, Billy got up from his seat, handed her a red rose corsage, and kissed her on the lips. It wasn't a heavy-duty kiss, but it was nevertheless a kiss. Mrs. Quirk, the English teacher, almost lost her teeth. The class hooted and whistled. Tad pulled at his shaggy hair. Angel rolled her eyes. Jessica cried real tears. Billy blushed.

First Mate, who'd beaten Jessica to the door, saw only chrome and sleek fenders. It didn't matter to her that Billy's bike was for a boy. She could swing her leg over the bar. She pictured herself parking Billy's bike front-end-first in the bicycle racks. She saw herself lock the bike, actually lock it up with a long chain and a big key and then stick the key in the pocket of her new Neiman-Marcus slacks. She'd wear the slacks with a silk blouse, like Angel's, and maybe a velvet vest. Her long brown hair would be in a real French braid, no more ponytails, not for her.

"Teenage dysfunction," Angel whispered as First Mate took her seat.

"Huh?"

"Adolescent crisis. Billy can't help himself."

"Oh. Right." First Mate murmured, dragging herself back to the real world.

"If the lovebirds would take their seats, I might be able to continue this lesson," Mrs. Quirk said.

The lovebirds were lucky. Mrs. Quirk had a sense of humor. She erased the compound-complex sentence from the board and copied the poem, "How Do I Love Thee?" by Elizabeth Barrett Browning.

"How do I love thee? Let me count the ways."

The bell rang. First Mate followed Angel to the door. Mrs. Quirk's sixty-four dollar vocabulary word for the day was tacked under the fire drill directions . . . incongruous.

"Incongruous–adj., absurd, unusual, strange. . . ."

First Mate and Angel were definitely an incongruous-looking pair of best friends. First Mate's brown hair was pulled tightly from her face and hung in a scraggly ponytail. Angel's French braid was perfect. Two little braids on each side melted into a thick plait tied with red velvet ribbon that matched her vest. First Mate wore a gray sweat suit. Angel wore red velvet pants. Angel's blouse was silk; her shoes the latest style. First Mate's canvas deck shoes were scrungy.

Angel wore a touch of lipstick and a bit of color on her cheeks. First Mate was pale as a whitefish. Today, her eyes were gray. Tomorrow, if she wore a blue sweat suit, they'd be blue. Angel's eyes were always brown.

Tad caught up with them.

"I think Billy's gone over the edge," Angel said, sadly. It was hard to lose a good friend.

Tad ignored her.

"I got a good price on some old computers. I need them for parts," he told First Mate.

She glanced around for any teachers. They always stood watch in the halls during change of periods.

"I know I'm up to my limit but I was thinking. Maybe I could work off another loan. It's not all that much money," Tad continued.

"Why don't you shout through a megaphone?" First Mate muttered.

"What? . . . Oh, a megaphone. Why? Who can hear? Nobody's anywhere near us." Tad said.

That was true. As usual, First Mate and Angel were in the middle of nowhere . . . gobs of kids ahead of them . . . gobs behind them. It didn't used to be that way.

"I think they're afraid of me . . . the bank and all," First Mate said to Angel.

"Glad it's not your deodorant," Angel giggled.

"C'mon, First Mate. What do you say?" Tad asked.

First Mate's gray eyes twinkled.

"I'll tell you what. I need somebody to change my manure pails," she told Tad.

"Manure?"

"Yeah. Every couple of days I get a fresh supply from Angel. All you have to do is dump the old manure in PJ's garden, go to Angel's barn, fill up the pails with a fresh supply, and bring them back to the ark. It takes about twenty minutes . . . maybe more . . . not much, though."

"Stinks," Tad said.

"Sure does," First Mate replied. "That's why it's worth advancing you money I'll never see again. I don't know, Tad, I pay you five dollars a week for the science homework that I don't even want, and you still need money. What's that aerocar made of anyway—gold?"

"Have you any idea what Alexander Graham Bell went through before he invented the telephone? Did you know that Igor Sikorsky, who invented the helicopter, had to sell his own company to Wall Street barons because he was broke?" Tad asked.

"Do you want the manure deal or not?" First Mate snapped.

"Oops. You're in a snit. I guess you didn't have time for breakfast again," Angel told First Mate.

"My mother always makes oatmeal. I hate it," First Mate grumbled.

"Then eat at my house. This morning we had home-made bread with strawberry pre—"

"Don't tell me. I don't want to hear what you had. It will give me a headache," First Mate cut in.

Miss Sally Stein, Angel's housekeeper . . . no . . . her nanny . . . no . . . her mother . . . no . . . the lady who'd taken care of Angel since she was two, and her own mother had died. Miss Sally was a wonderful cook. Even breakfast was a happening when Miss Sally made it.

In science class, Angel managed to slip half a sandwich to First Mate. That kept her going 'til lunch, when Angel emptied her lunchbox onto the table in the cafeteria with more sandwiches, raspberry tarts, and a box of chocolate covered cherries.

The card in the box read, "Happy Valentine's Day to my favorite kids, Angel Wilson and First Mate Tate."

That's the way Miss Sally was.

"I wonder why she never got married," First Mate mused.

"Then she'd have to leave me," Angel told her.

43

"What's she going to do when you grow up?" First Mate asked.

"Marry Jan Van Kluge and have a bunch of babies."

Like Angel's father, Jan Van Kluge worked all over the world. He and Miss Sally had met two years before, when he was in Shadow Lawn investigating an international diamond scandal. (Jan worked for Interpol.) The two of them hit it off like honey and pecans, which happened to be Jan's favorite cake, and for which Miss Sally had a fabulous recipe.

Jan was a little older than Miss Sally, but not too old to make them a pair because Miss Sally had been through quite a lot in her thirty-some years. When she was fifteen, the courts sent her to stay with Dr. and Mrs. Wilson. Angel wasn't born yet. She came along a year later and two years after that, Mrs. Wilson died. Sally had been crazy about Mrs. Wilson. She adored Angel. She stayed on to take care of her.

"Jan's in Nevada. We're going out there during spring break," Angel told First Mate, popping a chocolate-covered cherry into her mouth.

Can I come with you? a little voice cried from First Mate's heart. What would she do during spring break? Deliver newspapers—lend money—collect money—count money—watch the kids—clean the house—do the laundry—stand in front of the mirror and practice hollering at her father?

The afternoon passed so quickly that before First Mate knew it, Iron Nail was on the public address system requesting "Miss First Mate Tate" to report to the office. Only then did First Mate realize that she had only five more minutes before dismissal. A glint very much like the glint in her father's eyes that morning, sparkled in First Mate's. Detention! You think you'll corner me. Good try, Miss Vail.

Deck shoes are perfect for tile floors. They don't make a sound. First Mate was down the corridor, at the lockers, in her pea-coat and cap, and out the Upper Grades door before Miss Vail announced her name a second time.

In the navy pea-coat, First Mate's eyes looked blue. They danced with the fun of Miss Vail's game. She pedaled her battered old bike down Locust Avenue, her cheeks glowing rosy cold. When she spun around to Woodmere Drive, her ponytail sailed behind her. She didn't slow down until she hit Jennings Street. That was her street, and she had to be careful, for her father might be gunning for her.

. . . on the other hand, maybe he's simmered down by now. He might not even be home. Maybe he's at the marina. Maybe he's at the big AC. In that case, he found the money First Mate hid in the purple angel. Bummer! In which case Mom will be with him. Impossible—she wouldn't leave us alone on Valentine's Day, First Mate decided as she pedaled home.

First Mate peeked around bushes to her garage. It was open. Both the family car and Daddy's truck were in residence. She wasn't sure if that was good or bad, so she hid her bike behind the bushes and sneaked around front to the porch.

She peered inside the living room window. It seemed to be okay. The furniture was in place. The new lamps were still in one piece. Then again, they were metal. Then again, the lampshades weren't crooked. They'd be crooked if Daddy had thrown the lamps around.

He must have found the money right away, she thought. They probably went down early, lost, and returned already.

Oh dear, in which case, he's going to be in a mood. Why isn't he at the marina? Go to work, Dad.

First Mate opened the front door as quietly as possible. She needn't have bothered being careful because her father was clearing out the kitchen cabinets the easy way. He was dumping everything in them onto the floor. The noise was enough to drown out the school band.

Daddy had not found the grocery money. Right after First Mate and the kids left for school, Charlie called with an emergency, and Daddy had to rebuild the burntout motor in a speedboat. Daddy knew better than to ask questions. He merely did as he was told and got out of there. At times like that, though, he needed to gamble more than ever, so again he searched for that money, hurling the Fiesta Ware from one end of the kitchen to the other.

The crashes were sounds of victory. First Mate had won. Her father wasn't able to discover her hiding place. She breathed a quick thank you to the angels and went into Grams's room and closed the door.

The delight was short-lived. Her father had started his search in Grams's room. The place was a disaster. He'd even pulled the box spring off the bed.

Whatever possessed her father to think she'd hide money in her grandmother's sacred room? Didn't he know that to First Mate it was a shrine? Everything Grams had owned was a holy relic. First Mate might be angry with her grandmother for dying, but she still adored her memory.

Grams's mattress stood on its side against the bed frame. Blankets, sheets, bedspread, and clean laundry were scattered on the floor. The top of the dresser was bare. Everything that was on the scarf lay near the armchair.

Suddenly, it got quiet downstairs. Mom said something First Mate couldn't hear.

"She lies," Daddy roared.

He'd moved to the living room. There was a thud. Then another. Then another. Dad was turning the furniture on its ears. First Mate's stomach growled.

I'm going to puke, she thought, but she didn't. Instead, she sat down and put her head between her knees. That always made the feeling go away. Then she got up and pulled Grams's box spring far enough away from the closet door to open it.

Her collection coat was in a heap on the floor. She couldn't remember if, when PJ had told her about Elizabeth, she'd dropped it—or had she hung the coat up? She knelt down and checked the pockets. They were empty. First Mate knew she'd put the envelopes in them. Did he take them? Again her stomach turned. This time she ignored it, at least until she found the envelopes under the coat. Could they have fallen out of the pockets?

That was possible, especially since the envelopes were pretty much in order. Dad would have thrown them all over the place. First Mate stuck them back into the pockets, this time really deep so there was no chance of them falling out again.

She put on the coat, which was actually a raggedy Eskimo parka. She checked for her flashlight, pen, and the leather pouch she used to hold the money. They were untouched.

I must have dropped the coat on the floor, she thought, which was a relief because if her father had found those envelopes, he'd know she was hiding money somewhere else. She sure was—a whole lot of money, but not enough yet to buy back the boat yard. Someday though, she thought.

The sound of a glass shattering downstairs caught her attention. It wasn't a drinking glass. The sound wasn't brittle enough for that. Her mother laughed. Then her father. They were back in the kitchen.

"Let's go, honey!" Daddy roared to Mom.

He'd found the money. The noise she'd heard was the angel breaking. First Mate's heart sank. Were the angels on her father's side?

She'd wasted enough time with all the nonsense

downstairs. She had to get a move on, or she'd never finish the collections . . . and visit Grams—she definitely needed to do that.

In her hurry, First Mate didn't see the old Coca-Cola bottle that she kept near Grams's Madonna. It went down with everything else, but the bottle didn't break. First Mate tripped over it. She caught her balance and picked it up.

I'll give this to Grams, she thought. She's going to be mad at me for never visiting, and I need *her* on my side, what with the angels and all. Anyway, Grams is better than an angel. I should have gotten over my snit long ago.

Finding the Coca-Cola bottle intact had raised First Mate's spirits. The bottle was an antique and very valuable, but her father didn't know that, so she'd won . . . sort of. She put the bottle in her pocket and headed out. Unfortunately, Mom arrived to clean up before First Mate reached Grams's door. Mom and Daddy always cleaned up the messes before they left for the casinos. They didn't like the kids to see the mess he'd made.

They were both startled, Mom a bit more because she didn't recognize First Mate.

"What is that ugly thing you have on?" she asked when she'd found her tongue.

"How could you let Daddy do this to Grams's room?" First Mate asked in return.

"Nevermind, I can put it back together. Oh dear! You're a sight. Is that your grandmother's parka? I thought I threw it out."

"You did. I took it back. I like it. I'm going to wear it, just like she did, when I take my ice-cutter trip to the Arctic," First Mate said.

"Well, not today. I need you to mind the kids. We're going to Atlantic City," Mom told her, picking up the dresser scarf.

"You can't do that. It's Valentine's Day," First Mate protested.

"The heart cake is in the oven . . . two layers . . . and Sally Stein's mocha icing is in the 'fridge. I made it, not Sally. She gave me the recipe."

Mom spread the scarf, then picked up a perfume atomizer.

"And what are you doing in that coat?" she asked distractedly.

"I'm going out," First Mate snapped. "You stay home. You're supposed to stay home. I'm supposed to go out. I'm a kid."

"I hate it when you get like this . . . so judgmental. You know I'm doing the best I can. It's tough, but please, Honey, give me some help here." Mom said, studying the Madonna's broken body.

"Ellie?" Daddy called from downstairs.

"Be there in a sec," Mom sang.

Something was wrong with the picture. First Mate's mother was smiling. She wasn't upset. She wasn't angry. She was out and out pleased.

"You lie," First Mate told her mother.

"I what?"

Mom didn't look up.

"You gamble with him," First Mate said.

Mom played with the shards of the Madonna.

"I have fresh tomato sauce and meatballs in the Crockpot," she said in a very even tone.

First Mate walked out.

5

Jimmy Juarez's payment was tucked neatly under a bush at the corner of Jennings Street. He'd borrowed ten dollars for a Valentine for Annabelle MacPherson. Why Jimmy was wild about Annabelle was more than First Mate could figure, but his crazies, like Billy's, were good for business.

First Mate checked his envelope. Nope. He didn't ask for more money. Too bad . . . maybe next time. She put the envelope in an inside pocket. Then, she scrounged out Jimmy's new bill. It took longer than usual because the envelopes weren't in order. She hadn't realized that some were still mixed up.

At last she found Juarez.

"2/21 - $9 due. Pay $1.80."

She looked around for a new hiding spot.

"Hole in the tree by this bush," she wrote, and set the new envelope where the old had been.

First Mate's parka blended perfectly with the dull gray afternoon. She kept her back to the street, so no one noticed her slip Jimmy's two dollars into the pouch. She made eleven more collections before she reached the florist shop. Inside, Mrs. Antony was fixing bouquets to go out. She looked sideways at First Mate.

"We don't give away no flowers," she told her.

"Do you have yellow roses?" First Mate asked.

Mrs. Antony looked again.

"First Mate? What you doin' in that ugly thing? Take it off. Your Gramma would die all over again if she saw you in it."

First Mate untied her hood and pushed it back. Mrs. Antony's eyes filled with tears.

"You look just like her. You're Margaret through and through."

Margaret was Grams, Margaret Veronica Kelly Tate. Mrs. Antony took care of her when Grams was little. Mrs. Antony had to be at least ninety. She went back to the days when Shadow Lawn was just another village . . . nothing fancy. That was a long time ago.

She was pretty okay for an old lady, though, just a lot wrinkled. That's all.

"You bringin' Margaret her roses?" Mrs. Antony asked.

First Mate nodded.

"'Bout time."

How Mrs. Antony knew that First Mate hadn't ever visited Grams's grave, First Mate couldn't guess, but then the old timers seemed to know everything that went on in town.

"How you doin' in school?" Mrs. Antony asked, sharply.

She knows already, First Mate thought.

"Fine," she replied.

"You're very smart, just like Margaret was. I bet you're just as hardheaded."

First Mate smiled. "I need a dozen yellow roses."

"She was the only one who stood up to the Captain, and he loved her for it," Mrs. Antony continued.

"She missed him too much," First Mate muttered.

"She didn't die for that. It was her heart. Margaret always had a bad ticker," Mrs. Antony said.

First Mate blinked her tears away. She felt like a fool. "Do you have the roses?"

Mrs. Antony went to the refrigerator. "Half a dozen," she told First Mate. "That's all I have left. Three for me and three for Margaret."

First Mate slipped her finger into the money pouch. "How much?"

"Nuttin'. For my Margaret, they're free." Mrs. Antony wrapped the three roses. "And tonight when I put mine in the vase, I'll pray that things get better for you."

"Things are just fine with me, Mrs. Antony." First Mate mumbled, taking the bouquet. She put twenty dollars on the counter and left.

First Mate gently set the roses into the battered bike basket and flew down the street. She had a few more stops before Grams. At last she reached the path through the woods that led to the cemetery. She slowed down and turned in.

At the clearing, First Mate dropped the bike and gaped

at the tombstones. There were so many of them. Was the cemetery this full two years ago? So many dead people.

The Tate plot was halfway to the top of the main hill. First Mate took the roses from the basket and followed the frost-white path until she spied the tops of two sails. That was the tombstone, a granite boat with two sails, one for Cappy and one for Grams.

Grams's grave was filled in now, and grass grew over it. The frozen grass sparkled under the late afternoon sun. First Mate circled the part she remembered as a big hole with a coffin on top. She laid the roses on Cappy's side of the boat and pulled out the Coca-Cola bottle. She'd break the ice with him.

She swallowed, cleared her throat, and swallowed again.

"Hi," she said, weakly. "I brought Grams her yellow roses for Valentine's Day. Mrs. Antony says 'hi,' too."

She waited for a hello back, but none came.

"Are you both mad at me?"

Actually, First Mate had never heard Grampa talk. Grams was the only one who heard him when she and First Mate visited his grave.

First Mate pulled the coat tighter around her body. For the first time wearing this parka, she was cold. Her hands were almost too stiff to fix the roses in the bottle.

She turned to Grams's grave.

"It's worth a lot of money," she told Grams. "It will be worth more when I'm eighteen. I'm going to sell it back to the Coca-Cola Corporation."

First Mate wished Grams would answer. The silent treatment made her nervous.

"At least we knew when you were going, Cappy. Grams just upped and dropped dead on us! Imagine that —and left me holding the bag."

She felt bad about having to tell her grandparents about Daddy losing the boat yard. She felt worse having to tell about Mom.

"She's caught the itch," First Mate whispered. "I don't know why I didn't see it before today."

First Mate played with the roses a bit, then put them on the base of the tombstone.

"There's no sense being mad at me forever, Grams. I didn't do anything. You're the one who broke your promise. Remember? You said you wouldn't die 'til we all grew up. Cappy heard you, too. You said it right here in front of him."

Again there was silence.

"And by the way, I don't like the way you're not answering me. Maybe I don't love you the way Cappy does, but I love you. The least you could do is say hello."

A tear fled to First Mate's lip. She licked it away.

"Anyway, I brought you the Coca-Cola bottle. It would have helped me buy the boat yard back, but you're more important."

First Mate swallowed another lump in her throat.

"What I'm saying is I need you, Grams. You've got to help me."

She moved the flowers closer to Grams's side of the tombstone.

"Grams? Don't you hear me?"

First Mate hadn't considered what to do if her grandmother wouldn't talk to her. She'd like to wait until Grams got glad again, but she couldn't. She had the collections to finish. Come to think of it, Grams didn't know about Tate Bank. There was so much that she didn't know anymore.

There wasn't much daylight left. The sun was already falling toward the horizon. First Mate gave it one more try.

"I admit that I was awfully mad at you, but I gave that up because I had to. There's no sense playing games. I know you're not upset with me. You never stayed mad at me for more than two minutes, and I've been here for—" First Mate checked her watch, "—twenty-five."

She waited five long minutes.

"Do you hear me? I need help. I asked the angel on the windowsill, but Daddy broke it. I was wondering . . . do they have angels in heaven like the ones on TV?"

The tears fell so quickly that First Mate couldn't block them. How stupid of her! What ever made her think that her grandfather had actually answered her grandmother's questions when she visited his grave? Dead people don't talk. Grams had lied.

And I believed her. I'm an idiot! I'm the dumbest person in the world!

First Mate pulled the yellow roses from the Coca-Cola bottle. No more make believe. Her grandmother had tricked her once. Her grandmother had tricked her twice. There wouldn't be a third time.

"I'm all alone. I don't know what to do, but I'll figure it out, somehow."

First Mate threw the roses on the ground and stumbled down the hill. What a waste. What a ridiculous waste of time. She stuck the bottle back in her pocket and picked up her bike.

She had to pedal slowly because she couldn't see through all those tears.

6

Winter afternoons were chilly enough, but the night wind howling in from the beach made it impossible to ride a bike. There wasn't much First Mate could do about it. She walked the bike and held the parka close to her body, so she wouldn't blow away. She had changed her route to go to the cemetery. What a waste.

Her eyes burned. Whether it was from crying or the wind she didn't know. It didn't matter. Now and then, she blinked away a tear. It seemed to freeze on the way down.

A moving van passed. Its noisy motor blocked the sound of the waves pounding on the beach across the street. It would be so easy to cross over and jump into the ocean. The van was already around the bend and out of sight. There wasn't anybody else nearby. No one would see a girl in a funny coat disappear.

She'd leave the bike at the edge of the water and dive in. High tide would swallow it up. In school the kids would cheer because they didn't have to pay on their loans. But then they'd feel bad because there wasn't anybody around to lend them money when they needed it.

At home, the kids would eat the meatballs and the

cake. They wouldn't notice the mocha icing in the refrigerator. They'd watch some TV and go to bed. Mom and Daddy wouldn't pull in 'til the middle of the night. They'd go to bed, and then in the morning someone would call about not getting his newspaper. Mom would go upstairs. That's when she'd see First Mate wasn't home.

Mom would call Angel. Angel would say she didn't have a clue what happened to First Mate. Miss Sally would be upset. She'd call her boyfriend, Jan. He'd fly in with a whole bunch of Interpol agents. They'd look and look, but even the best wouldn't be able to find out what happened to poor First Mate Tate.

Her parents would have her picture put on milk containers.

"Have you seen this child? We can't gamble until she comes home.

Emily First Mate Tate
Age:12
Height: 5 foot 4
Weight:"

She didn't know. She hadn't weighed herself in so long.

"Weight: kind of thin, nice figure.
Eyes: blue, sometimes gray, sometimes the other way around.
Last seen at a cemetery in Shadow Lawn, New

Jersey, making a fool of herself talking to a tombstone."

Billy's mother was an artist. She would make up flyers to hang all over town. Mom and Daddy and the kids would ride around and hang them up on telephone poles. There might be enough flyers to hang on poles in other towns along the shore. Daddy'd be getting the itch. He had to get down to the big AC. Where was that kid?

Every Sunday all the churches would pray for the safe return of Miss Emily First Mate Tate. The synagogues would pray on Saturday. There was a mosque in Freehold. They'd pray, too. First Mate didn't know whether that would be on Saturday or Sunday. She'd have to look up the Moslem religion on Angel's Internet.

Finally, First Mate reached her last collection, the Great Jessica McLean's at Ocean's Edge. The halogen streetlights made the complex brighter than the boardwalk in the middle of summer. She stopped to adjust her eyes.

A windbreak of double evergreens offered enough protection for her to ride the bike again. She hopped on and pedaled to a big bush in front of one of the houses, not Jessica's. She stayed away from Jessica's place.

She hid the bike behind the bush and crossed the cobblestone street to the windbreak. Jessica's envelope was six trees down . . . on the beach side. Why did First Mate ever pick the beach side?

Because no one could see her there. Now wasn't that

stupid? No one was ever home at Ocean's Edge. At least no one seemed to be home. The place was one beautiful set of haunted townhouses.

First Mate pulled out her flashlight and squirreled under the sixth tree. A branch caught her parka. She took it off and regretted that immediately. Was it cold! She focused the light on the pine needles, running her fingers in even rows until she felt the yellow envelope. She picked it up and crawled back to her coat. She freed it from the branch and crawled out. She didn't see Billy standing across the street. He'd watched her crawl under the trees.

"First Mate?"

Billy crossed the street. He looked terrible.

"What's the problem?" First Mate asked, zipping up the parka. It was so nice to be warm again.

"She's gone," Billy said.

"What are you talking about?"

"Jessica. I came down to give her the rest of her presents. Nobody answered the door. The house is all dark.

"Maybe they went out for dinner," First Mate said, heading for her bike.

"No. I mean the house is empty. The curtains were down, so I looked in through the window. The den's empty. All the furniture's gone. I looked in the kitchen, too. There's nothing there but some newspapers on the floor."

First Mate stopped. "You're putting me on."

"I wish I were," Billy said. "See for yourself."

She followed Billy up the street to Jessica's. He was right. The curtains *were* down from the picture window on the porch. First Mate clicked on her flashlight and pressed the light against the glass.

"Damn!"

They ran to the back and checked the kitchen. It was empty, too.

"Is there a way we can get in here?" First Mate asked.

"I don't know," Billy said, trying the door.

It was open! What a dumb thing to leave your door open. They went inside and turned on the lights. The kitchen was cleared out—not a thing in it except a half-finished liter of soda in the 'fridge. The cabinets were empty.

The dining room was empty, too. Nails that had held pictures were still in the walls. The study, the den, the bedrooms upstairs were the same. Jessica and family were gone.

"You know, I saw a moving van on Ocean Road. I was kind of surprised 'cause trucks don't usually use that road, especially at night with all the wind. But then I didn't really care." First Mate told Billy.

They were in Jessica's room, pink flowered wallpaper and white wall-to-wall carpet. It smelled of Jessica.

"Let's get out of here." Billy said.

They turned out the light and went downstairs. They walked through the empty rooms one more time before they left. Billy locked the back door. It was the least he could do.

First Mate pulled Jessica's payment from her pocket and opened it. Twenty-three dollars and fifty cents.

"I've been had! She still owes me two hundred eleven dollars and fifty cents," she told Billy.

She wanted to say that she never liked Jessica, anyway, and she should never have lent her a penny, and she was glad Jessica had sailed out of town even if she did leave First Mate holding the bag for $211.50, but Billy looked so downhearted that she kept her mouth shut. They trudged to the front of the townhouse.

"You okay?" First Mate asked him.

Jessica's presents were on the porch. He climbed the steps and pulled a huge heart-shaped box from the bag.

"How'd you like to buy a box of the best Belgian chocolate?" he asked.

"Valentine's Day! The kids!" she cried.

7

Christopher, Ferdy, Barry, and Elizabeth sat in the den sharing a layer of Valentine cake. The television blasted. Mr. McGoo guarded the mouse hole in his living room. Ferdy finished his cake and got off the sofa.

The kitchen smelled like spaghetti sauce. Ferdy climbed on a chair and checked the Crockpot. His mouth watered. He climbed down and pulled the chair to the dish cabinet, but there weren't any dishes, so he found some paper plates in the pantry and fixed himself four meatballs and a pile of spaghetti sauce.

Back in the den, Mr. McGoo was gone. Spiderman climbed up the Empire State Building.

"We're not supposed to touch the meatballs," Elizabeth said.

"We weren't supposed to touch the cake, either," Ferdy replied.

He stuffed meatball number one into his mouth.

"Wonder what happened to First Mate?" Barry asked.

Who cared? Christopher, Barry, and Elizabeth left Ferdy with Spiderman and headed for the kicthen. Ferdy had left the paper plates on the counter. They all found spoons and helped themselves.

First Mate found them on the sofa, mouths dripping red sauce.

"You monsters," she howled, charging across the floor. She slammed off the TV. "Who said you could eat, and who said you could eat in here? Look at the mess you made . . . tomato sauce all over the place. Get up! Clean up! Get this stuff out of here! What do you think . . . I'm your servant?

"You see what I mean, Grams? I don't know where you are, but you see what I mean? I could use a little help here, if you don't mind."

The kids scrambled like ants, picking up paper plates and spoons, running them to the kitchen, chasing back with sopping wet dish towels that dripped all over the place, so First Mate had to wring them out and then get the mop and wipe up the floor herself.

All the while, she mumbled and grumbled about how spoiled they were, and how they got away with everything, and how she was going to tell Mom what they had done, and they would be very sorry because she was going to make sure that Mom got good and mad and whapped them with the wooden spoon, which was what she got when she was a kid before Mom started reading books about how to raise kids and let them do whatever they wanted, and that was too bad because First Mate was sick of it all, and by the way it was Valentine's Day, and did anybody think about that? No, they didn't. They just watched television and dirtied the house so First Mate would have to come home and clean it, and she wasn't cleaning up after them anymore. So here were the silly Valentines, and they could pick out whatever they liked because she wasn't going to bother to sign them.

First Mate pulled from her coat the envelope full of cards that she'd raced to buy before the drug store closed. She hurled it into the den.

"So you hippogriffs sign your own cards while I go upstairs to eat all the candy I bought for you because you ate half the cake without waiting for me, and then you messed with the meatballs! Do I care?

"And if you don't know what hippogriff means, look it up in the dictionary, if you can read, *cause it's a monster*!"

Ferdy and Barry could read, but Elizabeth and Christopher were still learning.

PJ arrived from the cellar. He'd been working on Valentine's Day presents with an old jigsaw he'd found down there. PJ had cut out everybody's name in fat, round letters from the prettiest wood in his father's woodpile. He'd glued each name to a napkin ring. The names were beautiful, sanded smoothly and ready for paint.

PJ had set the presents ever-so-carefully at each place on the table. He figured that First Mate would shut up when she saw them.

"I suppose you made *your* mess in the cellar. Are you waiting for me to clean that, too?" she grumbled.

"There isn't any mess," PJ replied.

"We'll see," First Mate snapped, storming down the cellar steps.

To her surprise, there wasn't a mess, at least no trail of tomato sauce and cake crumbs.

"'Course there isn't," PJ told her when she returned. "I didn't eat. I was too busy finishing the presents. I've been working on them since Christmas."

Although he bit his lip almost clear through, PJ could not stop the tears from spilling. Embarrassed, he sat down and buried his face in his hands.

"Oh dear," First Mate sighed. "I didn't mean to hurt your feelings."

She sat down next to him, pulling her chair close enough to give him a hug, but PJ would have none of it. He pushed her away.

"I've got a big mouth, PJ, a very big mouth, and sometimes it gets carried away with itself," she told him, studying her chapped hands. "I didn't mean it. Honest . . . I didn't mean to make you cry."

While PJ let the last of his tears fall, First Mate studied the round, smooth letters of her name. He'd done a wonderful job.

"How did you make them?" she asked.

"I don't know. I just did," PJ replied, taking a paper napkin from Elizabeth. He blew his nose.

"I guess you've got the Tate talent for wood. You'll take over the boat yard, someday."

The others agreed. PJ had the gift. That was certain,

and everyone, even First Mate, was in awe.

He *will* run that boat yard. I'll see to it, she told herself.

When First Mate put the water on for her and PJ's spaghetti, the others decided they were hungry again. She wanted to tell them to starve, but remembered it was Valentine's Day.

"Okay," she said so pleasantly it scared them.

She dumped out the little pot and poured water into the big pasta pot. She told the kids to set the table, but they said the dishes were gone. She told them to use paper plates like the ones they'd put the meatballs on.

There were plenty of knives, forks, and spoons. They weren't breakable. First Mate had the kids wash the dirty spoons. While they were in the kitchen, she went to the den and found the bag of Valentine cards. She took it to Grams's room, locking the door behind her.

She dug into her coat pockets for the candy bars. She pulled out the Coca-Cola bottle and for the time being stored it under the bed. She separated the candy: Chocolate for PJ, Christopher, and Ferdy. Licorice for Elizabeth. Gummy Bears for Barry. She took off her coat and threw it on the bed.

It took a while to find red ribbon. In the search, First Mate found some white tissue paper. She wrapped each candy package and tied it with a bow. After that, she signed the cards.

"First Mate, the water is all boiled. Can we put the *ghetties* in?" called Barry from the hall.

First Mate had two more cards to sign.

"No, you might spill the water and burn yourself," she said.

"Can PJ?" Barry asked, jiggling the doorknob.

"I'll be right out."

Elizabeth joined Barry and the two pounded together on the door.

"Cut it out, you two!"

First Mate stuffed the money pouch in the bottom drawer of her grandmother's dresser.

"Do you kids want your candy or not, 'cause if you don't, just keep right on banging that door," she hollered as she closed the drawer.

"Hippogriffs," she grumbled, picking up their presents. "That's a great word—hippogriffs."

The kids had found Mom's mocha icing in the 'fridge and spread it an inch thick on the remaining cake layer.

First Mate poured some olive oil into the water and waited for it to boil again. Then she poured in two pounds of spaghetti.

By the time everyone sat down, it was almost nine. First Mate hoped against hope that her parents would arrive to make a fuss over PJ's napkin rings. She noticed him stealing glances at the door and felt sad. He was only ten. It wasn't fair.

"Daddy's got a big deal going. He's selling a boat to Donald Trump," she told PJ.

"Who's Donald Trump?" Elizabeth asked.

"A billionaire."

"Does that mean we get to be on TV?" she asked.

"Yeah, *Nickelodeon*." First Mate grinned, winking at PJ.

After the cake, there were the baths, and after the baths, there was the homework. But First Mate had too much work of her own to do, so she forged an excuse for each kid on Mom's note paper.

Dear Teacher, First Mate wrote, carefully curling the *T* and *D* as her mother did.

Please excuse PJ for not doing his homework. He wasn't feeling well.
> *Thank you,*
> *Ellie Tate*

and so on and so forth for Ferdy, Barry, Christopher. Elizabeth didn't yet get homework. She only carried a book bag because it made her feel important. The boys waited in line for their notes.

"A hug," First Mate commanded each in turn, "and remember the note is our secret. If you tell anyone, I won't be able to write anymore!"

The little ones fell asleep as soon as their heads hit their pillows, but PJ tossed and turned. He was so excited about his napkin rings. First Mate promised she'd wake him up as soon as their parents got home.

By and by, even PJ fell asleep. First Mate checked each room, kissing each sleeper on the cheek to make sure no one was playing tricks. Then she went to her room in the attic and stuffed her bed with extra pillows from the closet shelf. On her real pillow, she placed the wig

Billy had given her for a payment last Halloween. Mrs. Beak's wig was a lighter brown than First Mate's hair, but in the dark, who could tell? Her parents weren't very smart. They never checked with a kiss on the cheek.

First Mate tucked Cappy, her sailor doll, next to the wig and tiptoed downstairs.

It was well after 11 P.M., and her real work was just beginning.

8

Although she wore Grams's warm parka, First Mate shivered as she hurried to Noah's Ark. Not even the pouch in her pocket, stuffed with the money she'd collected this afternoon helped to lighten her spirit. Again, Grams couldn't comfort her.

Perhaps she was just so tired that her body couldn't produce any more heat. She'd had two helpings of spaghetti, but it felt like weights in her stomach. The trip to the cemetery weighed as much on her heart.

First Mate reached the staircase to the Ark and clicked on the flashlight. Tad hadn't started his manure-collecting job yet, so she had only five steps to worry about. It was just as well. She wasn't in the mood for checking trip wires. As she climbed, she held the coat close to her body, so she wouldn't trip on it.

The staircase circled the tree, ending at the gate to the deck. First Mate pushed it open and turned off the flashlight. She could open the padlocks on the portal with her eyes closed. She untied her hood and pulled out the keys she kept on a chain around her neck. She opened the portal and let herself in, quickly shutting the door behind her. She didn't bother to throw the inside locks. She was safe at this time of night.

First Mate checked the tarpaper on the galley portholes. She'd just replaced the old tape because it had become brittle in the cold. The new tape was holding. No one would see if she turned on the lantern, which she did, and pulled a container of milk from the 'fridge under the counter. She poured milk in her dirty cup and set it on the hot plate. Cocoa would warm her.

While the milk heated, she went inside to the playroom and again made certain her tarpaper was in place. This was the largest of the three rooms in the Ark. It had four portholes and built-in shelves and furniture. When First Mate was satisfied the portholes were blacked out, she turned on the two lanterns Tad had hung for her.

Immediately, the room came to life. First Mate smiled at all the pairs of stuffed animals sitting on her shelves. It was as if they waited for her—the Dumbos, the Curious George family, Mr. and Mrs. Panda, the Cheshire cats, the Donald Ducks, Mickey and Minnie Mouse, not to mention tigers and dogs and cats and teddy bears and so many more friends whom First Mate had wisely refused to give away.

"And the Lord said, 'First Mate needs animals to save from the flood. Let us take her to Disneyland, so her Daddy can buy some.'"

First Mate sat in her office chair on wheels. He was so much fun back then.

The milk boiling over on the hot plate brought her

back to the present. She jumped up, ran to the galley, and pulled out the hot plate plug. Immediately, the bubbles disappeared. First Mate took cocoa powder from the cabinet and dumped some in the hot milk. She mixed it with her pen. She used her sleeve as a potholder while she carried the cocoa into the playroom.

"Cheers," she told her friends and took a sip.

Ouch! Too hot! It burnt her lips. She set the cup on the desk and went to work, pulling the pouch and envelopes from her pockets.

First Mate sorted the money and counted it twice before she rolled herself to the stateroom, a tiny place with built-in-bunks and a huge chest with a handle carved in the shape of a pirate's face. He had a glass eye and a gold earring. First Mate pulled on the earring and the lid swung open. That was Cappy's gift for her sixth birthday.

The toys she once stored inside the chest now filled the bunks. In their place were stacks of paper money and rolls of coins. First Mate had amassed a fortune since that first loan to Tad Robertson. By this time next year, she hoped to double, maybe triple that amount. She might have enough to "give Charlie an offer he couldn't refuse." That was a good line. She'd seen it in a movie. She'd make it work for her.

She took from the chest her ledger, a bag of loose cash and change, money wrappers, and new envelopes. She put them on her lap and rolled herself back to the playroom, where she emptied everything onto the desk.

The cocoa had cooled. First Mate hoped it would untie the knot in her stomach. She drank it down in one long gulp. It didn't help, but it did warm her insides. She rubbed the cold out of her hands and counted the day's take.

It was wonderful. One-half of all those dollars was pure profit. First Mate bundled the cash and rolled the coins. Carefully, she noted the total in her ledger. That was the easy part. Now, she had to copy the totals from the envelopes to the client pages. When she saw those totals, she'd know to whom she could lend more money tomorrow.

First Mate had a few dozen requests stuck in the back of the ledger. Almost everybody wanted more money, but not everyone could afford it. Some kids had borrowed up to their eyebrows. She put the envelopes in alphabetical order and went to work.

The slam of a car door awakened her. A second door slammed. First Mate checked her watch. It was after 2 A.M. Her neck was stiff, her hands numb. She pulled them inside the sleeves of her parka and listened. Her parents were home.

Did he win? Did he lose? How bad was it?

First Mate got up and turned off the lanterns. Then she opened the porthole nearest the driveway and listened for the sound of the garage door hitting the cement. If she could hear it, Daddy lost. If she couldn't, he won.

She counted off the seconds . . . sixty, and no sound.

Eighty, and no sound. Then she heard the unmistakable ripple of laughter. Mom was laughing! He won!

First Mate closed the porthole and celebrated with another cup of cocoa. When she finished, the knot was finally gone from her stomach. It was awful waiting for her parents to get home.

She picked up her pen and went back to work. Maybe Daddy broke the bank. Maybe he didn't, but she still had a business to run.

9

At 5 A.M. the hard rock blasted from First Mate's radio alarm. She lay on top of her quilt, snuggled in Grams's coat and hugging her sailor doll, Cappy. She didn't remember going to bed.

The alarm-clock noise could awaken the dead. First Mate didn't like hard rock, but it was the only thing that got her up—at least until she reached over, turned off the radio, and fell back to sleep.

She was at a party. Angel's father, Dr. Wilson, was there. Angel stood in a party dress next to him, ringing the dinner bell. Miss Sally and Billy carried an enormous cake into the room. It had white icing and blue letters. "To our dear—"

First Mate couldn't read the rest. Angel was ringing the bell too loud.

"Angel, stop that. Will you stop? I can't hear myself think!"

First Mate sat up, wide-awake. Her second alarm clock clanged from the desk across the room. So that was Angel's dinner bell. She got up and shut off the alarm, then turned on the light. Wearily, she pulled off the parka and threw it in her closet. Then she tiptoed downstairs.

Shivering, First Mate dragged the bundles of newspapers into the front hall. Quickly, she closed out the frigid morning. She took a sharp knife from the hall closet and slit the bands around the paper bundles. Then, hoping Mom had remembered to set the coffee maker, she went for her first cup of java.

Yes! There was a God. Well, maybe not, but at least there was coffee. First Mate poured herself a cup, threw cold water on her face, poured milk into the coffee, and sugared it. Normally, she'd take the next few minutes to put on her shoes and socks. That gave her time for the coffee to cool. However, she hadn't taken off her shoes and socks last night, so she didn't have the minutes to cool the coffee. She blew on it, took a sip, and hurried back to the foyer.

In a half hour, the papers were folded and packed into two huge canvas bags, which First Mate dragged, one by one, into the kitchen. She finished her coffee, dragged the bags outside and dropped them one by one on the skateboard invention she'd concocted to get them to her bike and in the basket. There was no way she could pick up one of those heavy bags.

Another few minutes and First Mate was on the road, tossing papers left and right to imagined targets on her neighbors' welcome mats. She was good. She had to be. Papers on welcome mats brought big tips.

The crowd is on its feet cheering, "First Mate Tate!" First Mate swings her arm around and around and then lets the ball fly.

"Strike three!"

The crowd goes wild. "We've won. We've won. State champions!"

Dreaming kept her mind off the cold. By daylight she was back home. Mom was in the kitchen making oatmeal.

"I'm going to Angel's for breakfast," First Mate told her.

"Oh darling . . . darling . . . sweeheart. You're such a wonderful child. I don't know what I'd do without you."

First Mate remembered, *That's right, Daddy won.* She didn't dare let on that she knew.

"Lucky last night. Huh?"

"All because of you. We took every penny. We took the biggest chance in our lives. We closed out your whole account and went for broke!"

"My money? I thought you had the grocery money," First Mate said.

"Well, we did, but your father knew that wasn't enough, not at the craps table, and he had such a hunch. So we went to the bank and withdrew the newspaper account," Mom explained.

She took soup spoons from the drawer.

"Ma, that's every penny I ever made since I was born!"

"I know. I know. My heart pounded so hard it's a wonder you didn't hear it at home. You should have been there. Somebody new rolled. I never saw a man shoot dice the way he did. I don't think they turned once in the air. Anyway, the man kept hitting your father's bets! Every time he hit, your father gave him

80

a thousand-dollar chip, and then he'd hit again!

"The place was in an uproar. Pit bosses . . . crowds of people shouting and cheering. Then, your daddy bet every chip . . . every one of them. He went for broke! The man took the dice. The whole crowd held its breath. It was one collective silence!

"The man rolls. The dice fall! The crowd lets out a roar!

"We're rich again!

"La cucaracha! La cucaracha!" Mom danced around the kitchen. "Some men brought in two racks with six shelves each of five thousand dollar chips! I never saw so many chips in all my life. We followed the men into the back office and the manager counted them out. Honey, we'll never be poor again!"

"You got enough money to buy back the business?" First Mate asked.

"Well, I hope so."

Mom poured herself another cup of coffee.

"You going to pay me back the money you took?" First Mate asked.

"With interest!" Mom smiled, kissing her on the cheek.

"Good. Ten percent. And I want my own account. No co-sign anymore. We're going to change banks."

Mom danced back to the stove. First Mate went upstairs for a shower and clean clothes. She met her father in the hall. He threw his arms around her.

"Matey, you're the pride of the fleet!"

After her shower, First Mate packed the day's loans.

Three floors down, Daddy and the kids sang at the tops of their lungs.

> The Glendy Burke is a mighty fast boat
> With a mighty fast captain, too.
> He sits up there on the hurricane roof,
> And he keeps an eye on the crew.
> I can't stay here for they work too hard,
> I am bound to leave this town.
> I'll take my duds and I'll tote 'em on my back
> When the Glendy Burke comes down.
>
> Ho for Louisiana!
> I'm bound to leave this town.
> I'll take my duds and I'll tote 'em on my back
> When the Glendy Burke comes down.
>
> The Glendy Burke has a funny old crew,
> And they sing the boatmen's song;
> They'll burn the pitch. . . .

First Mate fixed her ponytail and headed off to Angel's. She took the front staircase.

    The nerve . . . closing out my bank account!

10

Miss Sally was one of those people who should have had at least a dozen kids. She mothered everybody in the neighborhood, but especially First Mate. That's because First Mate, being mama to her brothers and sister, needed mothering most of all.

It amazed Miss Sally that First Mate, who was so very smart, actually believed that her parents' trips to Atlantic City were top secret. First Mate was born in this town. She knew that a secret here was merely something nobody talked about.

Talk was gossip. It came from the mouth. Secrets were told in people's eyes. A secret was the hasty exchange of glances between two neighbors watching First Mate chase after the kids on a Saturday afternoon. A secret was a wary look from a clerk when Ellie Tate said she'd pay the bill with a check. A secret was a sharp glance of the commuter paying the toll north on the Garden State Parkway while Ellie and Pete Tate pulled into the south tollbooth. Even Miss Sally, who'd only lived in the town for three years, could read more secrets in her neighbors' eyes than she'd like to admit she knew. So why didn't First Mate see the obvious?

For breakfast, Miss Sally whipped up western omelets and sourdough biscuits to match Angel's Valentine present from Jan. It was a western outfit, a doeskin skirt and vest to match. The vest was embroidered with turquoise beads. The blouse was of different Navaho colors, mainly turquoise and red. Miss Sally liked breakfast to match whatever Angel wore.

Except Angel arrived in sweats. She wanted to dress more like First Mate. After all, they were new best friends.

Miss Sally had a fit. "Since when do you wear sweats to school? You don't even wear them to ride the horses!"

Of course not. Angel had two magnificent riding outfits, one English and the other American western.

"How are First Mate and I ever going to be sisters if our clothes are so different?" Angel asked.

"Your hearts are the same. That's what matters," Miss Sally told her.

She couldn't say more because First Mate was at the door in sweats and that awful pea-coat.

"I'll change if First Mate changes," said Angel.

"Change what?" asked First Mate, sticking a finger into the homemade preserves.

Miss Sally gave her finger a whack.

"Sit down and put the jam on a biscuit."

"Our clothes. I have lots of kilts. Want to wear one?" Angel asked.

First Mate laughed. "It won't go with my deck shoes."

"Kilts don't go with western omelets, either," sighed

Miss Sally, "but I suppose I can survive one mismatched breakfast."

If Ellie Tate couldn't take time to figure a way to get her daughter to dress right, Sally Stein would.

Billy came in while Angel and First Mate were upstairs. He looked sadder than yesterday's dirty socks. Miss Sally threw her arms around him. She'd missed him so. He hadn't been to breakfast, lunch, or dinner since September.

"You grew three inches at least," Miss Sally sang.

She dragged Billy to the measuring wall and with a cookbook on his head marked his height.

"I'm wrong. It's four. Oh, it's good to have you home again."

Miss Sally set another place at the table.

"I'm not hungry," Billy mumbled, sticking a finger into the homemade preserves.

Miss Sally smacked his hand. "Get out of that jam and sit down. A good breakfast will take your mind off Jessica."

She knew all about the McLeans skipping town. Who didn't?

Billy was embarrassed. He'd sort of snubbed Angel and Miss Sally. It wasn't that he'd wanted to, but Jessica never had a friend who was a boy, unless of course it was a *boyfriend*. She didn't understand that Angel was just Billy's very good friend. She was jealous, so Billy had stayed away.

He sat in his usual seat at Miss Sally's table, as if five months had never happened.

"Why would the McLeans sneak out of town?" he asked Miss Sally.

"Are you sure they sneaked out?" she asked.

"Jessica didn't tell me she was going to move. She knew I'd be at her house after school with her presents."

"Did she do anything to clue you that something was different in her life?" Miss Sally asked.

First Mate's omelet was ready. She gave it to Billy.

"No," he said, reaching for the ketchup. "At dismissal I said, 'I'll see you later,' and she said 'in a while.' She and her little sister got in the car, and they rode off."

"Does her mother always pick her up from school?"

"Usually Jessica takes the school bus, but sometimes her mom picks her up . . . when they're going somewhere. I mean when they were going somewhere."

"It sounds to me like Jessica didn't know she was going to move away," Miss Sally told him.

Angel and First Mate came in wearing kilts and leotards with pull-over sweaters and button-down collar shirts. Angel had lent First Mate a pair of leather shoes. First Mate's hair was in a French braid like Angel's. She even wore a little make-up.

"Very preppy," Miss Sally nodded.

"Nice. You look nice, First Mate," Billy added.

Angel didn't need a compliment. She always looked good.

The girls had taken too much time upstairs. They had to gobble down the omelets. Miss Sally fixed them a bag of biscuits and jam and drove them to school.

"I don't want you to be late," she said.

"I would never, never, never, not in a million years be late for school. Oh horror of horrors," First Mate said so seriously that even sad Billy had to chuckle.

School buzzed with rumors about the McLeans. Someone said that her father said that Mr. McLean owed money all over the place. Since Tad's father owned the bank, he knew that to be a fact. His father was at the bank now going over the McLean accounts.

Somebody else said that Mr. McLean was a big gambler, and that he was into a bookie for a pile of money. Somebody else said he owed money to a loan shark, and somebody after that said that Mr. McLean's ski accident last Christmas was no accident, that the bookie and the loan shark broke his legs.

"What do you know about loan sharks and bookies? Duh!" First Mate asked.

"Uh . . . wake up. We *do* live on the Jersey Shore. Duh!" came the reply.

The town had all kinds of stories about Italian Mafia and Russian Mafia and Colombian Mafia and Irish Mafia and any other nationality of Mafia that happened to be on television that week. Most of the "dons" lived in Jersey, or so it seemed. Of course, no one in school had ever actually met a Mafia person, at least no one owned up to knowing one.

First Mate found herself breaking into a sweat. It must have been the heavy wool sweater. She wasn't used to it.

In class, Tad moved his seat next to Billy. He wasn't

Jessica, but he was better than an empty desk.

First Mate passed out the loans. At lunch, she picked up nine new customers. She would have picked up eleven, but two seventh graders didn't recognize her without a sweat suit and pony tail. By two in the afternoon, she couldn't hold her eyes open. Mr. Schulsky gave her detention for snoring. She fell asleep again, so he put her out of class. Miss Vail passed her by in the corridor. She didn't recognize First Mate, either.

First Mate went to her locker, got her pea-coat and walked out of school. She walked and walked in the opposite direction of Jennings Street. She found herself near the beach. She pulled her cap over her ears and stuck her hands in her pockets. Her pea-coat wasn't as warm as Grams's parka.

If she knew her way around town, and she did, there would be a church a block down. It wasn't First Mate's church, but that didn't matter. She needed to talk to God. Unfortunately, the church door was locked.

Of course the door is locked, she thought. I'm forever shilly-shallying about whether or not there is a God. God's not a potato head. He won't open the church door for a shilly-shally.

First Mate turned around and walked home. By then, school was out long enough for her brothers and sister to be home, but they weren't. The house was empty. She was just as glad. She was too tired for all their song and dance. She went upstairs.

"I can't take it when things are up. I can't take it when

things are down. What's my problem?" she asked Cappy. The nice thing about telling him her problems was he'd never tell anyone else. "I'm so tired. No, I'm not tired. I'm scared. I'm so scared, and I don't know why."

First Mate awakened to the march of the Tate brigade stomping up her stairs. Worse than that, they sang that ridiculous "Glendy Burke," and Daddy wasn't leading, so they were all off tune. First Mate buried her head under the pillow.

As if the kids would let her keep her head under a pillow.

Barry led the parade in a brand new sailor suit—an admiral, no less, with all sorts of gold bands on his sleeves. PJ, Ferdy, and Christopher wore regular suits and new shoes and new shirts and ties. Elizabeth pranced around in a white fur coat and hat!

"Just like the one you wore in the picture!" she told First Mate.

There was a picture downstairs of First Mate in a fur coat and hat with a muff to match. She was about six, Elizabeth's age.

Mom followed with boxes from Neiman-Marcus.

"Get the rest of her stuff," she told the kids.

The boys bounced down the stairs. Elizabeth posed in the mirror.

"After all, I'm named after a queen. I can't go fetching here and fetching there," she told her "two" mothers.

First Mate opened one of the boxes. Under the tissue paper was a velvet pants suit much like Angel's. The second box held a pair of wool slacks and the same sweater First Mate dreamed about the day Jessica's big heels landed on her toes. The wool was as soft as Elizabeth's curls.

That wasn't all. The boys brought up boxes and bags and more bags and more boxes.

A sailor dress, kilts, more slacks and sweaters, button-down-collar shirts, skirts, blouses, leotards, silk underwear. (The boys giggled at that.) There were shoes, also, five pairs!

"How do you know my size?" First Mate asked her mother.

"Sally Stein told me. You have the same sized foot as Angel."

The last Neiman-Marcus boxes held four miracles: a velvet dress, a satin and lace dress, a coat for going to fancy places, and a brand new school coat!

First Mate looked at her mother with wonder.

"How did you know? How did you ever know?"

"That you wished you could have nice clothes?" her mother asked.

First Mate nodded. A frog clogged her throat, so she couldn't talk.

Mom reached for First Mate's hand.

"I was twelve once. I know that seems impossible to you, but I was once just a little girl," she murmured.

"Ma, I'm not little. Elizabeth is little," First Mate said, pulling away.

She wasn't used to Mom taking her hand. She wasn't

used to being touched or hugged or kissed. It made her uncomfortable. She played with the buttons on her fancy dress coat.

"First Mate needs a hat," Elizabeth cried. "We forgot to buy her a hat."

"There's a little girl in you, and there's a little girl in me, and when Elizabeth is older than I am, there'll still be a little girl in her," Mom told First Mate.

Her voice was softer than it had been in so long a time. It caressed more gently than her hand had.

She's beautiful, First Mate thought, like a real-life Snow White. Her skin so white, her cheeks so pink, her hair so dark, her eyes so clear and brown. She reached out to return the touch her mother had offered only a few minutes before, but at that very moment Mom got up and headed for the door. The magic was gone.

Then she turned back.

"Daddy's taking us to dinner. Wear the velvet dress. It makes your eyes blue. And wear the fancy coat." she said.

Elizabeth followed her mother down the stairs. The boys were long gone from the bedroom. Their voices rang from the kitchen.

"Ho for Louisiana!
I'm bound to leave this town.
I'll take my duds and I'll tote 'em on my back
When the Glendy Burke comes down."

First Mate hung her new clothes all around the room. The velvet pants suit went on hangers hooked on the top shelf of the bookcase directly opposite her bed. She stroked the soft velvet. I'll need a silk blouse like Angel's, she thought.

She draped the slacks and sweater over the night-table lamps, but she didn't like the look, so she hooked them like starfish on the wood trim above the closet door. She covered the three windows with the fancy coat and the two pretty dresses. The school coat, naturally, dangled on the metal arm of the floor lamp next to her desk— not that First Mate ever used the desk for school, but the coat looked like it belonged there.

When she was all finished, she sat on the bed and admired her treasures. Her focus moved from velvet to silk to soft wool. She pictured herself in each outfit, then got up and danced around the room holding one and then another in her arms.

Was this a dream? Was this heaven? She slipped the school coat on and checked herself in her mirror. It was plaid, mostly blue and green. Her eyes graduated to blue-green. They were a pretty color, but different. She'd never noticed green in her eyes before.

Oh my! Yes. First Mate had seen that blue-green twinkle in her eyes . . . that other time . . . when was it? Daddy was gone for two days, and then he came home with all kinds of money stuffed in his pocket. No, they both came home. Mom was with him.

Was that last year? NO! It was seventh grade. Grams was dead, already. Mom kept calling from Atlantic City. She said if she didn't stay with Daddy, he'd go bonkers.

That was the first time First Mate minded the kids for more than one day. She told Elizabeth that if she wet her pants one more time, she'd have to walk around without any underwear. Elizabeth stopped wetting her pants that weekend. Too bad First Mate couldn't get her to stop wetting the bed.

Then the two of them came home, Mom and Daddy. They were dancing and hugging and kissing. Daddy pulled out a wad of money and told Mom to go buy the kids some worthy duds.

First Mate studied the plaid of her coat. Mom bought the same plaid that time, but a vest, with a pleated skirt and a green sweater to match the green in the plaid. Mom said she'd suddenly taken a "deep and pervasive adoration of the color green."

First Mate took off the coat and watched her eyes return to gray. From somewhere near her heart, that old terror emerged.

It happened in autumn. The whole family went to dinner at the Inn. Everybody said what beautiful children the Tates were. Smiles glowed. Elizabeth was so good. She didn't even have a tantrum.

"*Ho for Louisiana. . . .*" They were singing up a storm when Daddy pulled into the driveway.

"*I'll take my duds. . . .*"

Daddy stopped short. The song ended. A strange man stood on the front porch. He looked scary—ugly—nothing like any of the boaters.

Daddy tried not to show that he was scared, but his

eyes betrayed him. He got out of the car and told Mom to park it and go inside.

Mom pulled into the garage. She told First Mate to mind the kids and went right into the house. First Mate let them play in Noah's Ark. She kept peeking out a porthole. The trees weren't so high then. She could see through the kitchen windows Mom pacing back and forth.

Daddy went somewhere with that man. Mom cried so hard that First Mate had to put the kids to bed. When he returned, First Mate was lying on Grams's bed listening to Mom cry.

Her parents spoke softly at first. Then Mom's voice sharpened like a carving knife.

"Why didn't you tell me that you owed him so much money? How could you do this to us?"

A shock ran through First Mate's body. That was the night her father sold the business!

First Mate dumped the coat over the desk chair. After a while, the trembling stopped. She was exhausted. Her head weighed so much she couldn't hold it up. She crawled under the quilt and grabbed Cappy.

11

The Inn was a four-star restaurant, written up just last summer in *New Jersey* magazine as "the *creme de la creme* of dining experiences at the Shore." Dinner at the Inn was a happening. Valets in tuxedos parked cars. Doormen in tuxedos escorted guests to a dining room where a *maitre d'* in a tuxedo greeted them before he sent them with a waiter or waitress also in a tuxedo to the table where a bus boy in a tuxedo poured water and brought out soft, fresh rolls and butter patties shaped like daisies. About the only men not in tuxedos were the ones who came to dinner.

"First Mate?"

Mom's new suit had a mandarin collar and round brass buttons embossed in an oriental design. It was a money green. Her hair was brushed away from her face, and her dark eyes sparkled. Her cheeks glowed.

The Tates always made the best entrance at the Inn. No other family boasted six beautiful children. Mom couldn't wait to show them off again. Everyone in the room would watch her darlings stroll like princes and princesses to the large table that once was strictly the Tate's for Friday night. Six waiters would seat the children. They'd sit ever so straight. Mom would smile at the nods of approval from all around her.

First Mate curled like a kitten in bed, her arms around Cappy. She was dead to the world, out to the count of ten. A tidal wave could have splashed over the house, and she'd have floated peacefully away.

"First Mate, wake up. You're late!" Mom cried.

First Mate didn't hear her.

"Wake up, child!" Mom cried, shaking First Mate.

First Mate ducked under the pillow. Mom shook her harder.

"Go away," First Mate mumbled, pulling the quilt over the pillow.

Mom yanked them both off.

"Let me alone!" First Mate cried, covering her eyes from the sudden light.

She was fully dressed, but she felt naked. She trembled with cold.

"I can't believe it! You're still in your sweats. Get up, girl. Get dressed!"

First Mate didn't budge. Mom's voice rose.

"Honey, your father's downstairs. The kids are itching to be fed. What's with you?"

First Mate peeked between her fingers.

"I think I've been run over by a moving van. I'm so tired, Mom. I can't go anywhere."

"Turn around. Let me feel your head," Mom commanded.

First Mate obeyed.

"You don't have a fever."

"No. I'm not sick. I'm just so tired," First Mate sighed, pulling the quilt back up over her head.

She groped for Cappy.

"But we're going to the Inn," Mom said, as if those magic words would stir First Mate to action.

"Go without me," she mumbled from under the quilt.

"We can't. It's Friday. This is a family thing," Mom said.

"Since when are we a family?" First mate asked.

"What?" Mom asked.

First Mate uncurled herself, pulled the quilt from over her face, and looked up. Her eyes re-adjusted themselves to the light.

"I said, will you please go without me? I'm exhausted! I want to sleep. I don't want to go anywhere."

Mom took First Mate's velvet dress from its hanger.

"Hurry up. Get this on. I'll fix your hair in the car."

First Mate didn't move.

"Get up. Did you hear me? Get up!" Mom demanded.

Her lips wore that little pout Daddy loved so much when he was in a good mood.

"This is all *déjà vu*," First Mate said.

"What?"

"*Déjà vu. Déjà vu.* We've done this before and we'll do it again," First Mate repeated.

"I know what *déjà vu* is. I don't know what your problem is," Mom replied acidly.

First Mate pushed the pillow behind her.

"You are my problem," she snapped. "One day you don't have money to buy a gallon of milk. The next day you're taking us all to the Inn. The *Inn* of all places. You can't pick up the menu there for less than fifty dollars—apiece that is!"

"What's that to you? You're not paying the bill," Mom said.

"I'm sure not, not since you cashed in my whole bank account," First Mate said.

"Please, make the snit later. Let's get going," Mom said, but First Mate didn't budge.

"And what are we supposed to do when you and Daddy get the itch and lose what ever is left of what you just won? You can't come to me, not even for groceries. I don't have a bank account anymore," First Mate continued.

Her voice rose sharply with every word. Her mother's was equally as sharp. The old carving knives were out and about.

"Is that what you're mad about? Your bank account? My Lord, girl, we won a hundred times that chicken feed you called a bank account. I spent as much on the clothes you threw all over the place. What a mess. You might have been nice enough to hang them in the closet where they belong!"

Mom was in full fury, but so was First Mate. Her money might be chicken feed in her mother's eyes, but it sure came in handy when she and Daddy lost. Chicken feed? Well, her mother didn't get up before the sun every morning to deliver 125 newspapers. She didn't pedal from one end of town to the other, rain or shine, cold or hot, on a bike that should have been scrapped before First Mate was born, so the family would eat three squares a day, even when Mom, who had lied and said she only went to the casinos to stop Daddy from gambling, when in fact, she couldn't get down there fast enough to gamble the grocery money, the electric bill, and anything else she or Daddy felt like shooting across that craps table. . . .

"I don't do craps. I play my slots," Mom corrected.

"Slots? You mean you throw quarters down a . . ."

"Stop! Not another word! I can't believe what I'm hearing! How dare you. How dare you call me a liar! How dare you talk to me like this! You're not even thirteen years old. You don't have a clue what life is all about. *You're* telling *me* how to live mine?

"Stay home and feel sorry for yourself. We don't need your sourpuss at dinner."

Mom hung First Mate's velvet dress in the closet and stormed from the room, but not before First Mate hollered.

"What's Charlie Fisk going to take next? The house? I'm pretty sure that's all we've got left."

First Mate jumped out of bed and ran to the stairs, shouting over the clatter of her mother's heels on the steps.

"We used to be rich, you know, not that I knew it then, but I sure know it now! And by the way, I think it stinks to have a mother who lies. At least Daddy doesn't lie!"

First Mate waited to hear the back door slam. Pretty soon it did, and she went back to bed, but then she got up to watch the family car turn up the street. From the attic, the car was nothing more than a toy in Christopher's collection.

For a while, First Mate stared down at the empty street. Then she jumped on the bed and sat cross-legged in the middle, glaring at the velvet pants hanging on the bookcase. She didn't like them, anymore. They were ugly. She looked at the satin and lace dress, the slacks and sweater, the coats.

They have to go back. They all have to go back. I've got to get money to start a new bank account. I can't take anything from Tate Bank.

The thought of her father working for that disgusting Charlie—in the business her grandfather started when her father was just a little boy—in the business that would fall on its face without her father taking care of things—it was almost too much to bear.

Every time First Mate saw Charlie at her father's desk, her stomach turned. Every time Charlie ordered her father around, First Mate wanted to scream. Every time she picked up her father's paycheck, she wanted to bite off Charlie's hand. The day would come when the chest in Noah's Ark held enough money to send Charlie packing!

Of course, I won't put the business in Daddy's name,

First Mate thought. It will be in my name. Daddy will be the boss again, but he won't be able to gamble away the profits.

In the meantime, she folded her beautiful new clothes and tenderly slipped each item into its box. Then she collected the sales slips from where ever she'd thrown them.

She added the prices mentally. Mom had lied again. The clothes didn't cost half of what she and Daddy stole.

12

First Mate jumped up and slammed the off button on the clanging alarm. Up and at it. She turned on the light.

The house was an iceberg. The temperature had dropped a zillion degrees overnight. First Mate slipped a clean sweat suit over her pajamas, dug her deck shoes from under the bed, stuffed some clean socks inside one of them, and made for the bathroom off the kitchen. There, she threw enough cold water on her face to remember today was Saturday! Big Money Day! One hundred and twenty-five fat tips for the best and only papergirl in town. She grinned at herself in the mirror.

The salty wind from the ocean was frozen with dampness that cut to the bone. Goose bumps prickled First Mate's body. Shivering, she hauled in the last bundle of papers and slammed the front door. Brrr. She turned the thermostat up twenty degrees. Daddy always set it at sixty before he went to bed.

She opened the bundles and scooched away the knife. Once, she'd forgotten and left the knife on the floor. Barry got hold of it and sliced his hand. What a mess. Blood all over the place. First Mate was out delivering papers. Mom and Daddy weren't home yet from the big

AC. Good thing PJ had enough sense to call Miss Sally. She took Barry to the hospital. He had ten stitches.

That's when First Mate learned how to clean up blood. Miss Sally poured peroxide over the stains.

"Let it sizzle before you dab it up. If you have a lot of blood, you might have to pour the peroxide quite a few times, but it takes the blood out of anything—if you get it while its fairly new."

Miss Sally knew a lot of good stuff like that.

Saturday papers were not all Saturday's. All the special Sunday sections hitched a ride with them. "Travel," "Education," "Entertainment," "Book Review" to name a few. Added to that were advertisement flyers, at least a million.

An act that big couldn't be folded like the dailies and tossed on porches. First Mate had to pack each newspaper in a plastic bag, then stuff them like shrimp into three canvas sacks, each of which weighed a ton.

She dragged the sacks, one at a time, into the kitchen. The coffee was ready. She filled her mug and added milk and sugar. Then she sat down to slip on her socks and deck shoes. That gave just enough time for her coffee to cool. She gulped it down, put on her ski mask and peacoat, buttoned the jacket, put on her gloves, and dragged each sack outside to the trestle.

Her bridge was a succession of boards nailed to two-by-four legs that ran from the second porch step to her bicycle basket. Quarter rounds served as tracks that held her skateboard in place, so she could roll a sack of newspapers right to the bike. (Her front wheel was wedged in place so it couldn't turn under the weight.)

When First Mate wasn't around, the kids rode her skateboard down the trestle. PJ could hit the sidewalk without falling and spin on to the driveway. Ferdy was pretty good, but Barry, Christopher, and Elizabeth generally bailed out before the skateboard reached the jump zone. There were more than a few bumps, bruises, and bloody noses, but nobody ever told First Mate about them.

First Mate reached Ocean Road just before sunrise. She stopped, got off the bike, and crossed the board-walk. She had only a few more deliveries to make, so the basket wasn't too heavy for the bike to lean against the rails. She sat on a bench and waited.

The surf was deafening. The sea gulls still slept wherever it is that sea gulls sleep, so no "swizzles," as First Mate called the sea gull songs, spoiled the thundering pulse of the water as it crashed and rolled, then recoiled on itself to crash and roll all over again. Waves smashed over sand and rock, and even at times the boardwalk, hurling a fresh salt spray onto First Mate's face.

The wind soothed her ragged feelings. It helped her forget how furious she was at her mother and father, and at Grams, and at God. She forgot how lonesome she was for the time when every single thing in her world didn't revolve around her parents' trips to the big AC, a time when she didn't worry about money or food or what her father would do when he again went crazy.

No, for those precious minutes in darkness, First Mate let herself be a kid sitting on the boardwalk waiting for the sun to rise.

The sky paled to purple. *Poco a poco*, bit by bit, little by little, the purple created an infinite number of pastels bursting from the point where sky met water. Hoops of fiery red and orange smothered the softer shades, then bowed in homage to the color rose, which guided the sun from the other side of the horizon to its throne above the town. The sun turned gold, then paled to white flame that burnt First Mate's eyes. She looked away. The day was born.

Sighing, First Mate hopped on her bike and pedaled across the boardwalk to the street. She jumped the curb and headed south. From the street, she couldn't see the ocean, but she still heard the waves clap and fall. The music wasn't the same, though. Its charm was gone. The salt air wasn't spice, either. It was ice biting her face.

First Mate delivered and collected at the homes on the other side of the road. It wasn't going to snow that day. The sky was too clear. The sea gulls swarmed over the water. Not one had ventured over land. Sea gulls always flew inland when it was going to snow.

Not that First Mate wanted snow. Snow was a pain. It was terribly difficult to deliver papers in the snow. On the other hand, snow was fun. You could roll in it, or sled in it, or throw it at people. Snow was pretty, too. It painted everything a glowing white, like clean sheets fresh from the dryer draped all over town.

First Mate turned into Ocean's Edge and stopped for her first customer. She ran up the steps of the townhouse, dropped the plastic-bound paper on the mat and collected the small yellow envelope tacked near the door. She didn't need to open the envelope. In fact, she never opened her Saturday morning envelopes until she got home.

Ocean's Edge people were pretty good with tips, not amazing, but not bad either. Jessica's father, Mr. McLean, had been almost amazing. Once, he'd left a ten-dollar bill for her, and it wasn't even Christmas! First Mate wondered how such a nice man managed to get stuck with such a nasty daughter.

She passed the McLean townhouse. Come to think of it, he owed her for most of the past week, chicken feed compared to Jessica's tab, but a dollar's a dollar.

Mr. McLean was a decent man. He might have remembered to slip her envelope in the mailbox before he skipped. First Mate turned the bike around.

The mailboxes were on the street. They were shiny brass with "OE" for Ocean's Edge stamped into the side in fancy letters. First Mate braked at Mr. McLean's and pulled open the door. The box was empty. He'd stiffed her. Bummer!

"Hey, what are you doing with my mail?"

First Mate didn't have to look up. She recognized the voice immediately—Charlie's. It scraped like chalk on a cheese grater. What was he doing here?

He stood in all his ugliness on McLean's porch. He was wrapped in a bathrobe, and his hair was wet. He must have just gotten out of the shower . . . *their* shower. What was *Charlie* doing taking a shower at the *McLean's?*

"I was checking to see if the owner of this house left his newspaper delivery payment," she hollered.

He probably wouldn't get pneumonia. He wouldn't even get a sniffle. No decent staphylococcus would bother with a man with so much badness in him.

"Yeah, well now this is my house, so get lost," Charlie snarled.

His house? Since when?

"Gotcha," First Mate called. "By the way, when did you move in?"

"What's it to ya?" Charlie asked.

"Not much. What happened to Mr. McLean?"

The question popped out uninvited.

"None of your business, kid," Charlie replied. "Now like I said, get lost."

Charlie slammed the door. First Mate studied the empty spot where he'd stood. How could the bank sell the house so fast? She'd have to talk to Tad about this.

Maybe Mr. McLean sold the house. Daddy'd said that Charlie was looking for a place closer to the business. He didn't like the long drive from Atlantic City.

Whatever peace First Mate had gleaned from the sunrise evaporated. She finished her collections and headed home.

13

Billy was already in the kitchen when First Mate and Tad arrived. Angel was upstairs changing her riding clothes.

"What is it today?" First Mate grinned.

"Western omelets. She wore the English outfit. It won't do," Miss Sally said.

"She's been up there for an hour. I'm getting hungry," Billy grumbled.

Actually, he'd only been in the kitchen for five minutes, but he was tired, and he still felt terrible about Jessica's sudden departure. Miss Sally had the omelets ready for the pan. She opened the oven, freeing the sumptuous smell of newly baked sourdough bread.

"Don't touch. You'll burn your tongues," Miss Sally told the boys.

"I'll see what I can do 'bout movin' Miss Angel along," First Mate drawled in as good a Western accent as she could muster.

The scent of the bread followed her to the third floor, where Angel was trying on cowboy hats. She was in the American West, naturally. That was one of the many suites on the third floor. Each had a bedroom, sitting room with an outside porch, and a bathroom.

The third floor wasn't always so swank. Back in the time of the Civil War, when the mansion was part of the Jennings estate, it housed the family's servants.

Dr. Wilson bought what was left of the old estate at a sheriff's tax sale. He needed a big place to store the artifacts and other objects he'd collected in so many years of traveling around the world. Miss Sally's job was to fix the place up and to help Angel plant roots in this nice little American town. It was time for Angel to settle down. She needed to belong somewhere.

Until then, Angel had always traveled with her father and Miss Sally. She had no idea what it was like to live in one place for more than six months.

At first, Angel enjoyed Shadow Lawn. Miss Sally had given her the whole third floor, so if she got bored, she could move from room to room, which she did. Each night she chose a different place to sleep. To let the day maid know what bed to make the next morning, Angel pinned a star to the door.

For a while, that was fun. Then Angel tired of her game. She missed traveling with her father.

"Why don't we fix up your floor? We can have a suite for every country you've visited," Miss Sally suggested.

"I'd rather be with my father," Angel replied.

"You need to plant roots," Miss Sally said.

"He doesn't. Why must I?" Angel replied.

"Because you do. Take my word for it," Miss Sally said.

Jan Van Kluge found the perfect interior designer, and

all last winter and summer the carpenters and the painters and the plumbers and who knows who worked on that third floor. There were the Chinese, the Japanese, the Indian from India, and the Egyptian suites. There were the Russian, the French, the English, the Moroccan, and the American West. There were the Hawaiian Islands and Australia. Angel's old star was replaced with a flag to represent every land. When she went to bed, she raised the flag. First Mate had only to see that flag, and she knew exactly where to find her friend.

"Hurry up. We're all starving," First Mate told Angel.

"I'm having such a hard time. I just don't know which hat to wear," Angel sighed, putting on the Stetson for the tenth time.

"You don't need a hat for breakfast," First Mate reminded her.

She loved being in Angel's world. It was so different from her own.

Angel took the Stetson from her head and put it on First Mate's.

"You look great in this. Why don't you dress West with me?"

"Because I'm hungry," First Mate told her.

"Oh come on. I'll fix your hair in braids."

"A French braid?" First Mate asked.

She loved French braids.

"Of course not. That's French. How about native American—two braids."

The next thing you know, First Mate was all done up in Jan's present, the doeskin skirt and vest. Angel tied her braids with turquoise leather thongs. She liked the outfit so much that she wished she had a second one for herself.

"You be the cowgirl," First Mate suggested, smiling into the mirror.

She put the Stetson on Angel's head and led her downstairs. Halfway down, First Mate ran back up. Angel had a million places to hide the newspaper money!

Next to the American West was China, and in China First Mate found a large vase to deposit her envelopes.

"Did you know that's from the Chou dynasty?" Angel asked.

First Mate jumped. She hadn't expected Angel to follow her back upstairs. She had no choice but to explain the situation, sort of.

"I need a place to keep my money, somewhere I can get it if I need it."

"Nothing better than that vase. It's from the time of Confucius. Put your fortune in my father's fortune," Angel grinned.

The bell at the end of the hall clanged. Miss Sally was getting impatient. Angel ran to the stairs and called down.

"We're on our way."

"Well hurry up before the boys eat me out of house and home," Miss Sally hollered.

To let Angel know she meant business, she pulled the rope to the old school bell one more time.

By the time First Mate and Angel arrived at the kitchen, Billy and Tad had finished the whole loaf of sourdough bread. Her omelets were to die for, though, and she whipped up biscuits for the girls.

"I did a little snooping about Jessica," Billy said, reaching for a biscuit. "The kids in school were right about her father owing money to a loan shark."

First Mate choked. Angel put her hands in the air while Tad beat her on the back. When she could breathe again, Billy continued.

"Mr. McLean gambles . . . a lot. Jessica mentioned it once, but I didn't pay much attention. Anyway, according to very reliable sources, Mr. McLean had markers out from every loan shark in the east."

"How could he owe so much money and be so rich?" Tad asked.

"My father was a gambler," Miss Sally said, pouring herself a cup of coffee. "The McLeans aren't rich. Take my word for it."

"Poor Jessica," Billy sighed.

First Mate hoped nobody heard her heart thumping.

"Miss Sally, will you drop me off at the mall, this afternoon?" she asked, wiping the beads of perspiration from her forehead.

"What about me?" Angel asked.

"Didn't I say you?"

"Nope," Angel replied.

"Well, I meant to. I'm sorry. Will you drop us both off?"

Miss Sally wasn't thrilled. She didn't like the idea of the girls "prancing around the mall with nothing more on their minds than the boys."

Billy and Tad hooted.

"As a matter of fact, I have to exchange a whole bunch of clothes," First Mate explained. "My mother bought them for me, but I don't like them, so I'm going to exchange them or maybe return them, if I don't find anything else I like."

"Won't it hurt your mother's feelings if you show up wearing the clothes she *didn't* pick out?" Miss Sally asked.

"Well, yes, but it would hurt my feeling worse to wear them," First Mate replied, evenly.

"What time do you want us to pick you up?" she asked First Mate.

"How 'bout three?" Angel suggested.

Three was fine with First Mate.

14

Elizabeth's sheets stank. She'd peed the bed again. What else was new?

"She's getting worse," First Mate told Mom, as they stripped it.

The rubber sheet was soaked. The mattress was wet around the edges of the sheet.

"Don't let her drink any water before she goes to bed," Mom told First Mate.

"How 'bout you stay home once in a while? She seems to stay dry when you're in residence," First Mate snapped.

"Do you want a house to live in?" Mom asked.

"Spare me," First Mate replied. "You're hooked as much as he is. You don't stop him one little bit. You just make sure he gives you money to play your slots."

Mom gave First Mate an odd look, but she didn't say anything. She took the rubber sheet into the bathroom to soak it in the tub. First Mate stood Elizabeth's mattress on its side and opened the windows. She hoped the cold air would dry it.

Elizabeth hadn't always wet the bed. It all started last year in kindergarten. She'd had a bad day. First Mate couldn't remember what happened, probably Elizabeth couldn't find the crayon she wanted. Whatever, she came home from school all teary-eyed. Mom wasn't home. First Mate had to make her Tate Bank collections. Elizabeth was blabbering and blabbering about absolutely nothing, and First Mate got mad and told her to get lost.

Elizabeth took her seriously. She walked all over town, but then she couldn't get lost because she knew her way home from everywhere, so she walked back home crying that she was sorry.

"Sorry for what?" First Mate asked.

"Sorry I couldn't get lost," Elizabeth wailed.

First Mate couldn't stop laughing. Then the boys came in. Elizabeth told them her tale of woe, and they started laughing. Everybody but Elizabeth rolled on the floor, screaming and laughing and then crying because they couldn't stop laughing. Elizabeth went upstairs. She wouldn't come down for supper. She cried herself to sleep. That night she wet the bed.

The way First Mate saw it, if Mom had been home where she belonged, the whole thing wouldn't have happened. On the other hand, First Mate felt guilty. She never seemed to know what to do with the kids. She could feed them. She could make sure their clothes were clean, and their hair was combed before they went to school. She could correct their homework and put them to bed, but she just couldn't take it when one of them started bawling about nothing.

First Mate went to Barry's Room. What a disaster. Dirty underwear, clean underwear, dirty socks, clean socks, dirty polo shirts, clean polo shirts, sneakers, shoes, toys, books, you name it all over the floor. It's a wonder the kid didn't kill himself plowing through to the bed at night.

First Mate picked up his new jacket and pants and hung them up. She found his tie hanging on the bedpost. She put that away and stripped the bed. She used the sheets as a giant mop, kicking them and everything in their path to the hall.

"Barry," she called downstairs. "Barry, come on up here and pick up your stuff. Barry?"

Barry was in the den watching the Saturday morning cartoons. It wasn't fair. It just wasn't fair.

"Barry, get your behind up here!" First Mate screamed.

Barry emerged at the bottom of the steps. He was still in pajamas. His honey-colored hair was tousled, and his lips were brown from the chocolate chip cookies Mom baked this morning.

"I'm watchin' *Mr. McGoo!*" he cried, astounded that First Mate didn't realize *Mr. McGoo* was the be-all and end-all of the entire world and then some.

"Yeah, well, you Mr. McGoo yourself right up here and sort out your clothes so I know what's clean and what's dirty. And while you're at it, put your toys and everything else where it belongs. I'm not Marcy, you know."

Marcy used to be their maid, but Mom had to let her go because she couldn't pay her.

"Can't you wait 'til *Mr. McGoo* is over?" Barry asked. Scowling, First Mate took a merciless step in his direction. Barry sprinted to the back steps. He knew better than to go back to *Mr. McGoo*, but he sure as shootin' wasn't going near First Mate. He tiptoed up the back stairs and peeked around the corner of the hall. First Mate was still waiting at the front steps. He waited until she got tired of waiting and went on to Christopher's room. Then Barry very quietly began the trial of sorting out his stuff. It seemed to him that he should be able to do anything he wanted with his own stuff. On the other hand, Barry didn't run the place, not yet.

Christopher's room put First Mate in a better frame of mind. He was a neatnik like she. He had a place for everything and everything was in its place. His clothes were in their drawers, his new suit hung in the closet, his toys were in the toy box, and his books were in his bookcase. Daddy was like that, too. Mom was a bit on the sloppy side, although nobody seemed to notice.

Which reminded First Mate that she hadn't seen her mother for some time. She wasn't in the bathroom, although Elizabeth's washed rubber sheet was drying on the shower rod.

"Mom?"

"Ma?" First Mate called.

She found her mother in the bedroom, sitting on her side of the bed and staring into space.

"You going to help me, Ma?"

Mom gazed at nothing for a few seconds more, then snapped out of it.

"Oh," she said to First Mate. "I was just thinking. I was in such a good mood, this morning. Why do you have to be so nasty all the time?"

"I'm not nasty," First Mate protested.

"You certainly are. You're the grouchiest person in this family. Daddy felt terrible that you wouldn't go to dinner with us last night. And then, this morning, you started hollering at me again. I just don't understand you, First Mate."

"Mom, Elizabeth is wetting the bed too much. I wasn't hollering. I was making a statement of fact," First Mate explained.

"She must be like I was. I wet the bed until I was ten years old," Mom replied.

"Did you start when you were five?" First Mate asked.

"How should I know? I can't think back that far," Mom said.

"Well, I found an interesting article about bed-wetting in one of the parents' magazines that you never read anymore. There's a muscle that controls the bladder. It's called the sphincter muscle. If a child wets the bed from the time she is potty trained, then there's a problem with the sphincter muscle. But if the child stops wetting the bed and then starts again at a later age, that's caused by trauma."

"Are you telling me that I traumatized Elizabeth?" Mom asked.

"I'm telling you that you and Daddy are traumatizing us all!" First Mate replied.

"There you go again. Now you're going to say I gamble. I knew you were going to drag gambling into this conversation one way or another. You should be grateful. Maybe we should take up drinking!"

Mom's eyes were pretty, but they were also crazy with that same gleam Daddy always got in his . . . the one that said:

"The lights are on, but I'm not here. Please don't notice."

It was scary.

First him . . . now her . . . who'll be next? First Mate thought. Now that was terrifying. Obviously, her mother had caught this gambling problem from her father. Did that mean *First Mate would be next?* Was gambling contagious? Did it come from a brain virus . . . maybe bacteria that attacked the brain? Daddy was a nice person before he went bonkers on gambling.

Grams must have known more about gambling than she ever let on. Did she know Mom would also get infected? She must have known First Mate wouldn't.

That's why Grams called me to the hospital and told me to take care of the kids, First Mate thought.

Well, there was no sense doing all this work to buy back the business if PJ was going to gamble it away again. In the meantime, First Mate would try to be nice.

Mom was sick in the head. She couldn't help herself.

"I love you, Mom," First Mate said, kissing her crazy mother on the cheek.

They changed the sheets, sorted the wash, and put the first load in the washer. Mom set the water temperature on cold, so First Mate would have plenty of hot water to take a shower before she went to the mall.

Mom was glad First Mate was going to have some fun. Maybe that was the problem. She did have to babysit an awful lot.

Daddy returned in high 'G' from the marina. He was so excited. He'd just sold a boat from under Charlie's nose.

"Did you know that he's moved into the McLean house?" First Mate asked her father.

"No," Daddy replied, pouring some orange juice in one of the new glasses Mom had bought yesterday.

"What are people going to say? As far as they know, Charlie works for you. Now he's moved into the McLean house."

"I don't get the point," Daddy said.

"You don't?" First Mate asked. She tried to keep the edge from her voice.

"No."

Daddy finished his juice.

"The talk around town is that Mr. McLean gambled —like somebody else I know. He gambled so much that he had to borrow money from loan sharks. He couldn't pay, so he skipped town."

"Damn it!" Daddy threw the glass in the sink so hard that it shattered. "Now look what you did. Well you can clean it up, Miss Mouth!"

He ran up the back stairs.

"Ellie? Ellie? Where the hell are you? Ellie? Let's get out of here."

The kids stood at the den door watching. Five pairs of eyes accused First Mate.

"Now look what you did."

Mom hadn't yet gone food shopping. There weren't any paper towels left, so First Mate used toilet paper to collect the shards of glass. Mom and Daddy walked downstairs and kissed the kids goodbye.

"First Mate is in charge. You do what she says, or else," Daddy warned them.

First Mate turned her back to her parents. They had no intention of kissing her goodbye. She'd had some nerve getting her father so upset.

Just before Miss Sally and Angel were due to pick her up, First Mate carried two enormous shopping bags to the back deck. Each was stuffed with her beautiful new clothes. She'd put the receipts in an envelope and stapled it to one of the bags. She waited for Miss Sally and Angel to pull into the driveway.

There they were, right on time. First Mate signaled Angel to lower the car window.

"I can't go," she called.

"Why not?" Angel asked.

"Come here a minute."

It wasn't hard to get Angel to take the shopping bags. She and Miss Sally would return the clothes.

"And put the money you know where," First Mate said.

"The Chou vase," Angel sighed.

"Thanks a lot. I mean it," First Mate said.

"Spare me," Angel replied, rolling her eyes in dismay.

First Mate watched Angel carry the heavy bags back to the car. She hoped the handles wouldn't break before Angel had a chance to return the clothes.

Miss Sally waved but didn't smile. Angel didn't even wave.

15

What First Mate wanted was an hour in her parents' Jacuzzi with a little bubble bath and the water jets on high, but giving the kids an hour alone could spell disaster, so she settled for a shower. PJ was in the cellar making birdhouses. He'd already sold a few around town. He didn't tell First Mate where he hid the money, but knowing PJ, it was very well hidden. The kid was smart! By next year he'd be ready to help her with Tate Bank. He could take over the operation at Ferris Antoon, while she handled the high school. There was a lot of money to be made in the high school.

First Mate put the last wash in the dryer and checked on the kids. They were curled like kittens in the den.

"You kids need anything, ask PJ," she told them.

Bang, bang, bang . . . PJ was really going at it down there. Why not? Daddy had started working on boats at ten. That's the way the Tates were. Make your money young.

First Mate didn't let herself think the rest—*then gamble it all away.* She knew she wouldn't do that. What about PJ?

She stepped into Grams's shower. It had a seat and

handles on the sides. First Mate sat and let the warm water flow over her body. It was almost as soothing as the Jacuzzi. She rolled her head, letting the water drip from her hair. Too bad she'd had to take out those nice braids, but this felt so good.

She rubbed her shoulders. The muscles were tight. Soon, they loosened. She wiggled her toes. That felt good. The knot in her stomach dissolved.

She squeezed a dollop of shampoo into her palm, then rubbed her hands together and began washing her hair. Her fingers moved evenly along her scalp, massaging and remassaging. When she got rich, she'd have her hair washed every day in a beauty parlor.

Her thoughts moved to the ever-present Sword of Damocles, or was it the pendulum that hung over her head as in the story she'd read in English class. Her father gambled. Now her mother gambled. Was this some sort of virus?

If it was, could it be cured? AIDS was a virus, and people took medicine to keep it under control. It wasn't curable but. . . .

Gambling was just as bad, it seemed, at least the way her parents gambled. Did everybody gamble like that? Billy's parents went down to the casinos sometimes. So did Tad's. Billy'd say, "They won. They lost. They had a good time." So did Tad. Why did their parents not get drunk on gambling?

First Mate rinsed the shampoo from her hair until the strands squeaked when she rubbed them against her fingers. She let more water pour on her face, then rubbed in the hair conditioner.

Come to think of it, she'd learned a lot in health class about the dangers of drugs, alcohol, and cigarettes. Why didn't the teacher talk about gambling? Why wasn't that in the health book? People who gambled too much *hung their kids out the window*. That was dangerous.

First Mate had to stop. Her stomach was in knots again. She soaped herself down and rinsed. Then she turned off the water and stepped out, wrapping herself in one of Grams's supertowels. It felt delicious.

She went to the hall and listened over the banister for sounds of trouble. All was peaceful in the den. Hugging the towel to her body, she went upstairs to blow-dry her hair.

First Mate brushed her long brown hair until it fluffed. She made her ponytail a bit looser, wrapping it first with a rubber band and then tying one of the turquoise thongs into a bow over the band. She found a sweater almost the same color in her drawer and put it on with a pair of jeans. At least it wasn't sweats. She pulled on the riding boots Angel had given her and went downstairs to check herself in Mom's full-length mirror. Not bad.

She brushed some of Mom's blush on her cheeks. Now, if Daddy drank, everybody in town would know it because he'd be slobbering all over the place. If he did drugs, it would be the same. First Mate put on lipstick, admired herself again in Mom's mirror, and ran down the back steps to check on the kids again. They were so wrapped in TV that they didn't notice her take out the encyclopedia. It was the G volume.

First Mate brought it to the kitchen, where she could read in peace, but the book only had one paragraph about gambling and then a whole bunch of REFERENCES. If she had to look up all those pages, she might as well go to the library. She brought the book back to the den.

"You kids watch too much TV," she said, turning it off.

"What's it to ya?" Barry asked.

He always had something to say. First Mate ignored him.

"Get your coats. We're going to the library."

"That stinks," Barry said.

"It does not. It smells like books," First Mate told him. "We're going to the library, and you kids are going to read for a change. Every book you read, you get a quarter, and don't bother reading any of those skinny little picture books because you don't even get a nickel for one of them.

"But I can't read yet," Elizabeth whined.

"That's true," First Mate agreed. "You and Christopher can do the picture books, but you have to try to read them. You'll never learn to read sitting here watching cartoons."

She sounded like Mom in the old days.

The afternoon was on its last legs. The town library would soon close. The university library stayed open later, and it probably had better information.

First Mate went to the cellar.

"I need you to help me with the kids, PJ. We have to go to the library. I have to look up this gambling. It's making me crazy."

"Why don't you leave them home with me?" PJ asked, sanding a finished birdhouse.

First Mate ignored the question. PJ was too young. Suppose somebody got hold of another knife? She couldn't insult him, though.

"I'm going to give each kid a quarter for every book he reads. Elizabeth and Christopher don't have to read, but they have to turn every page and try. Can you keep an eye on them? You know how they cheat."

"They can't do much damage watching TV right here," PJ replied, setting the birdhouse on the workbench.

"Oh ye of little memory," First Mate sighed.

They exchanged glances. PJ was about to pry open a can of paint. He put the opener down and followed his sister upstairs.

Outside, First Mate took the lead, PJ the rear. They played shadow all the way. Whatever First Mate did, the others had to copy. She jumped curbs. She did pirouettes. She touched trees and bushes. She walked in a zigzag pattern. She hopped. She skipped (until Elizabeth whined because she couldn't skip). Everyone followed exactly except PJ, who felt too important to act like a kid.

By the time they reached the library, First Mate was exhausted. She hoped that the kids were, also. Then they'd fall asleep, and she wouldn't have to dole out much money for the books they read. PJ took the kids to the children's reading room. First Mate headed for a computer in the main reading room.

She keyed in "gambling," and waited. To her surprise there were more listings than even she would be able to remember. She went to the desk and borrowed a pencil and a lot of paper. Even she wouldn't remember all the titles.

She started with microfilms of magazine articles. She found enough films to keep her busy and took them to a viewer. It cost a dime per article. She had plenty of dimes.

The first article said, "The excitement of gambling awakens pleasure receivers in the brain. The delight felt by the problem gambler is the same as a 'high' felt by a drug addict. For this reason, compulsive gambling is considered a disease."

First Mate wrote like crazy.

The next dime told her that 5 percent of all gamblers had a serious problem called Compulsive Gambling. That meant they couldn't stop gambling. They were caught in the thrill of the game. They didn't gamble to win. They gambled to gamble.

Which meant, as far as First Mate was concerned, that 5 percent of all gamblers gambled because it made them feel good. It sure did, but what about the other 95 percent? Did they gamble to feel bad?

First Mate scribbled more notes.

The third article was called "Causes of Pathological Gambling." Before she started, First Mate got a dictionary and looked up the word "pathological." Two meanings made sense. 1. PERTAINING TO OR CAUSED BY DISEASE; and 2. DISORDERED IN BEHAVIOR; *A PATHOLOGICAL LIAR.* So . . . pathological gambling was caused by disease. The disease wasn't an infection. It was a way of behaving.

Once she cleared that up, First Mate could read on. There were ten reasons for pathological gambling. The fifth hit First Mate like a sack of potatoes: "Some people begin gambling pathologically after the death of a family member."

That was Mom. She'd started after Grams died. Gambling must have made Mom feel good, which in itself was bad because it put Mom in the 5 percent of people who absolutely have to gamble. Now, if she were in the 95 percent, she wouldn't have felt so good, so she probably wouldn't have gone back. That was bad.

First Mate wrote down, "Grams's death = Mom gambling."

The next seven articles repeated what the first three had told First Mate. A few said that "studies were not conclusive," which meant the doctors who wrote the articles didn't know much. She tried one more article, and on the third paragraph, she froze!

"One compulsive gambler threatened to throw his son from a three-story window if his wife did not provide him with the money she'd hidden for the family groceries."

Pathological gamblers threw kids out of windows. What else did they do? Steal from their children? Lie? Borrow money and *get murdered*, or did they have a business to sign over? Did they get their legs broken? Did they skip town because they couldn't pay their bills?

How could gambling make a person happy when it caused so much misery?

First Mate read until her stomach hurt so much she had to stop. She rewound the microfilm and turned off the viewer.

She hadn't found a cure, but there was a way to get help. It was like Alcoholics Anonymous, only for pathological gamblers. They went to meetings and talked about all the misery they caused. It made them feel terrible enough to stop gambling.

Were there meetings like that in Shadow Lawn? Now that Mr. McLean was gone, were her parents the only problem gamblers in the town? She checked her notes. One of the articles had given a 1-800 number to call for help. She went to the pay phone and dialed it.

The number rang and rang and rang. First Mate waited and waited and waited. She hung up and dialed again and waited again and again and again. Was this another lie?

She was exhausted.

16

"I d-d-d-don't w-w-w-want to w-w-walk that f-f-f-far. I-I-I-I w-w-w-want to g-go home," Christopher said, as First Mate checked to see that his hat and mittens were on okay. It was a long walk to Sam's Pizzeria.

"Don't you want pizza?" First Mate asked him.

"Not if I h-h-h-have t-t-t-to w-w-w-w-walk," said Christopher. "I-I-I-I-I-I'm t-t-t-t-t-tired."

He stuttered worse when he was tired.

"I'll call Jeremiah. He'll pick us up in Petunia," First Mate offered.

"Really?"

"Really?"

"Really?"

"R-r-r-r-r-really?"

"Really?"

Five pairs of eyes danced with excitement. Even PJ couldn't contain himself. A ride in Petunia was worth walking a mile!

Petunia wasn't just a taxi. It was a 1937 spit-polished black Cadillac limousine with running boards and a horn that sounded like a tugboat's. A ride in her was an event . . . a happening . . . a birthday present. First Mate and PJ were the only two Tate kids who'd ever had the pleasure.

For First Mate it happened on her sixth birthday. Cappy made her the pirate chest, so Daddy needed to go one better. He called Jeremiah Cleary, who owned the taxi, and hired Petunia for the day.

First Mate, Billy, and Tad sat in the back seat. Daddy sat up front with Jeremiah. They drove all the way to the train station in Bay Head Junction. Marcy, Mommy's maid, was waiting there for them. She had a party all set up for the ride home. They took the train. Marcy served ice cream cake with six candles on it. Everybody on the train sang "Happy Birthday."

Daddy did it! He beat Cappy! The ride was better than the pirate chest. First Mate never said so, though. Cappy would have gone off for a couple of days. He did that sometimes. Nobody knew where he went. He always came home again, but Grams got so upset that it was better not to say that Daddy won.

First Mate checked her pockets for money. She hadn't stashed all the envelopes in Dr. Wilson's Chou-dynasty vase. She'd kept enough for emergencies . . . and then some.

All was a-okay. She had enough money for the taxi ride. She went back to the pay phone and dialed information for Jeremiah's number.

Maybe I should have called information for Gambler's Anonymous, she thought.

Jeremiah picked them up right away. He was tall and narrow with a ruddy face and curly gray hair. He never wore a hat, not even in the coldest weather, and that night was exceedingly cold.

PJ helped Jeremiah stash the kids in the back seat. Then he got in, but First Mate opted to sit in the front as her father had done on that winner birthday. A glass separated Jeremiah and her from the kids, which was a good thing because they opened the windows and hooted and hollered all the way to Sam's Pizzeria.

"Just like you used to do," Jeremiah grinned.

First Mate cringed with embarrassment.

"How do you remember? I only rode in Petunia that one time," she sighed.

"You rode in Petunia lots of times. I suppose you don't remember," said Jeremiah, puffing on his pipe.

"I never acted like those hippogriffs," First Mate snapped.

"Well now, isn't that a fine word. And would you be telling me what it means?"

He still had a touch of a brogue.

"It means *monsters*," First Mate snapped.

As they neared the Station, which was directly across the street from Sam's Pizzeria, Jeremiah rapped on the glass divider. PJ opened it.

"Settle down, now. We're near civilization. Your sister doesn't want to land with a bunch of *hippos*," he winked.

The kids burst out laughing. They knew the joke was on First Mate, but they did calm enough for her to hold her head up when Jeremiah parked Petunia.

The crowd was hip-deep in front of the pizza parlor. Everybody stopped talking and stared at Elizabeth, Christopher, Ferdy, and Barry, getting out of Petunia. First Mate was so embarrassed. Why did her parents have to have so many kids? Couldn't they have stopped with PJ?

She tried to lose herself and the kids in the crowd, but it was no go. Anywhere she stood, people moved away—and stared. First Mate would have liked to evaporate.

Elizabeth started sniveling, "I'm cold. I want to go home."

"Shut up," First Mate whispered in her ear.

"I will not shut up. I'm hungry," she wailed.

Everybody gawked. What was the problem? They all knew the Tate kids.

"How about waffles," First Mate suggested, pointing across the street to the Station.

"You said we could get pizza," Barry told her.

"I changed my mind!"

First Mate grabbed her littlest brother and sister and marched across the street. If the others wanted supper, they'd follow. If not, who cared?

The minute PJ opened the Station door, First Mate remembered that she'd forgotten something for the third time today! On Saturday nights, teenagers who didn't yet drive met at the Station to go to the movies. That meant the eighth graders, and half of them were already inside.

There was no turning back. She had to get these kids fed. Besides, she had such a lump in her stomach that if she didn't sit down, she'd double over. She stood by the wall and watched PJ lead the kids to a table.

The aromas soon settled her stomach. Hot waffles and toast, hamburgers and hot dogs, grilled cheese and bacon sprinkled their fragrances to every corner of the cozy room.

Tommy Callahan stood next to First Mate. They weren't bosom buddies, but she never expected him to suddenly move away from her. Oh well . . . who cared?

Angel and Tad always went to the movies. When she didn't have to baby-sit, First Mate joined them. Billy always took Jessica, but that was out now, so maybe he'd go with Angel and Tad.

As she scanned the room for them, First Mate noticed a lot of people staring at her. When she smiled, they looked away.

She went to the bathroom to check her makeup. It was fine, she looked good. Maybe that's why everybody stared. They never knew how pretty First Mate could be.

Ann Levinson left a cubicle and washed her hands.

"Did you see Angel?" First Mate asked her.

Ann stopped, stared, and finally said, "Uh . . . no."

First Mate wanted to ask, "Gee, do I look that good?" but she felt funny bragging about herself. She went back and found the table PJ had picked out.

"The waitress wouldn't take our order," he told First Mate.

"Of course not. You don't have any money."

"How does she know?" PJ asked.

"Because she does," First Mate replied, waving for some service.

The waitress took her time, but she finally arrived. They ordered waffles and homemade ice cream. First Mate asked for a loaf of garlic bread and a cocoa all around.

"Was she snotty, or was that my imagination?" First Mate asked PJ after the waitress left.

"No snottier than she was to me," PJ shrugged.

The restaurant became crowded. Various cliques claimed their territories. A few stood near the counter waiting for friends. By the time the waffles and ice cream arrived, the place was mobbed . . . no Angel and Tad, though.

First Mate ordered seconds on the waffles. PJ and Barry could have taken thirds, but enough was enough. First Mate went to pay the bill.

Did the kids around the cash register step away from her? Did everyone suddenly stop talking? Had somebody puked all over First Mate's head?

She paid the bill and went outside to wait for PJ and the rest of the kids.

Neil Rosetti's mother drove up in this year's BMW.

When she saw First Mate, she looked the other way.

"Now ye wouldn't be planning to walk those wee uns all the way to your abode on a night such as this. Would ye?"

Jeremiah Cleary's grin was as silly as his brogue. First Mate had been so busy noticing everybody snubbing her that she didn't see him approach.

"Your father called and asked me to drive you all home," he explained.

First Mate was surprised.

"He did?"

"He did. He'll pay me in the mornin'," Jeremiah nodded.

He was a terrible liar, but First Mate was grateful. She pretended she believed and helped PJ stow the little ones in Petunia. Again, she sat up front with Jeremiah.

They rode in silence for a few blocks. Then Jeremiah said, "So the word is out."

His brogue had suddenly disappeared.

First Mate stared at him.

"What do you mean?"

"You don't know?" he asked.

"I guess I don't," First Mate replied.

"I'm telling you right now that I don't believe a word of what I hear. Your Daddy's a fine man. I've known him since he was a tad."

Jeremiah changed Petunia's gear and turned onto Jennings street. "I'd never have brought the matter up if I'd thought for one minute that you didn't already know," he continued. "Now remember this, Little Lady, I'm on your family's side. Your father has his faults, and I suppose that's what's at the bottom of this mess.

"Whatever happens, you hold your head as high as you did tonight. Your grams would have been proud of you," said Jeremiah.

He slowed down, changed Petunia's gear, and pulled into the driveway. The garage was open and empty. The house was dark.

Jeremiah shifted to neutral and got down from Petunia. First Mate pulled herself together. The kids couldn't see her so upset. As Jeremiah helped the little ones out, he told PJ.

"Your sister's a good kid. Help her out."

"I do," PJ replied.

They weren't in the house five minutes when the phone rang. It was Tad.

"Where you been all day?" he asked.

"How come you and Angel weren't at The Station tonight?" First Mate returned.

"That's what we have to talk about," Tad said. "Can you come over to my place? My parents aren't home."

"Of course I can't. I'm minding the kids," First Mate replied.

"How about we go over there, then," Tad said.

"Meaning?" First Mate asked.

"Me, Billy, and Angel."

"Billy, Angel, and I," First Mate corrected.

"Whatever," Tad said. "We all need to talk. It's very serious. We've been friends too long to have something like this mess us up."

"Can you give me an hour?" First Mate asked, numbly.

She couldn't think. She couldn't feel. Her stomach didn't even hurt.

"The kids. I've got to get them to bed," she added.

17

PJ put the kids to bed. That is, he made sure they got their baths and then let them sit on their parents' bed to watch TV. After he left, they curled themselves under the quilt.

"If you need me, I'm in the cellar," he told First Mate.

She didn't reply. She was too numb. She sat as her mother always did, like a statue at the big table. If "this mess" as Tad had called it, was what she thought, there wasn't a thing she could do to fix it.

Angel, Billy, and Tad arrived on the nose of 9:10. Billy and Tad hadn't been to First Mate's house in some time. They wished the occasion were merrier.

They hung their coats on Grams's, and Mr. and Mrs. Tate's hooks. First Mate could only offer tea or coffee. Mom hadn't shopped yet. Tad took tea. Angel and Billy didn't want anything. First Mate poured herself a cup of coffee and led her friends up to her new room in the attic. That offered the best protection from prying little ears.

Billy and Tad were impressed. First Mate's new room was twice the size of her old one. She had four gabled windows and built-in shelves under all the eaves. The floor was made of decking from a yacht her father had demolished. It was painted baby blue, her favorite color. On either side of her big brass bed was a thick blue throw rug.

Angel and First Mate sat yoga-style in the middle of the bed. Billy and Tad opted for one of the rugs. There was no small talk. There was no kibitzing. Tad got right to the point.

"Your father's man, Charlie . . . did you know he moved into Jessica's house?" he asked First Mate.

"I saw him there this morning," First Mate sighed.

"Well . . . that pretty much puts the kibosh on you lending money to anybody else," Tad said, "even to me, and I feel awful about that."

"Run that by me again?" First Mate asked.

"There's a good chance that one of your clients has already told a parent that you're a loan shark, too. Loan-sharking is a federal offense, you know. Can your father cover for you?" Tad asked.

"My father cover me for what?" First Mate asked.

"For loan-sharking. Can you transfer that ledger of yours into his name?" Tad asked.

"Maybe you should burn it," Billy suggested. "And whatever you do, get rid of any other evidence you have. That way it will be the kids' word against yours."

It had taken Tad hours to get Billy on First Mate's side. He was so devastated about never seeing Jessica again that he couldn't separate First Mate from her father. He figured they were both in business together.

First Mate gouged the kids, while Mr. Tate gouged everybody else.

"I doubt Mr. Tate knows that she's got her own racket going," Tad had said.

"What makes you so sure?" Billy asked.

"Because she keeps everything locked in Noah's Ark. I put the locks on the door, and believe me Harry Houdini wouldn't be able to get in there. On top of that, she's got the steps booby trapped with enough manure to fertilize Third World agriculture. Why would First Mate go through so much trouble if her father was helping her?"

"Beats me," Billy said. "Maybe she wants to be independent."

"Yeah, maybe she doesn't like the fact that her father hurts people," Tad replied.

"Maybe she hurts kids. How do we know?" Billy argued.

"What kids?" Tad asked.

"We don't know who she lends money to."

"She lends money to us, and sometimes we can't pay. Does she hurt us?" Tad continued.

What clinched it for Billy was the fact that Tad would actually suffer if First Mate stopped lending him money. The aerocar was almost built. All he needed was money to buy a few more parts. But to Tad, no great invention was more important than a great friend, and First Mate had always been that.

"Remember when the bakery truck ran over my frog? First Mate went out and caught three more for me. I'll never forget that," Tad said.

"She was awfully nice about giving me a job so I could pay off the money I borrowed for Jessica," Billy admitted.

"And she can't stand Jessica. Now that's a friend," Tad said.

So Billy swallowed his heartache and went with Tad to tell Angel that First Mate was being investigated. Someone had told a parent about her loan shark operation.

"Loan shark?" Angel cried. "She's no loan shark. From what I can see, she keeps a lot of greedy kids very happy, excepting you two, of course. You're not greedy."

Angel couldn't tell Billy and Tad that she'd just returned all of First Mate's beautiful new clothes to some very exclusive stores, and that First Mate had asked Angel to hold on to the money. She couldn't say a lot of things because they were secrets. Not even First Mate knew that Angel knew them.

"If First Mate's in trouble, then we have to figure a way to get her out of it," Angel declared, so the three of them went over to First Mate's house, but nobody was home.

Tad's parents were at a shindig for the Monmouth County Historical Association. His mother was president this year. Since nobody was home to listen, he

could call First Mate's house every half-hour until somebody *there* got home.

Somebody finally did, and there they were—Angel,
Billy, and Tad in First Mate's new room. She was furious
at them. She uncrossed her legs and sat, straight as a
poker, on the edge of the bed.

"If you knew what a loan shark *really* was, you'd
never accuse me of being one."

"Like we don't know? Duh . . . remember Jessica?"
Billy retorted.

"To tell you the truth, I'm glad she's out of here. I
couldn't stand her. She turned you into a perfect nin-
compoop," First Mate snapped.

Billy stood up.

"I'm outta here!" He headed for the door.

"Wait a minute." Angel blocked his path. "We can't
start calling each other names. That's not going to help."

"I didn't call First Mate anything," Billy said.

"You called me a loan shark!" First Mate groused,
to which Billy replied, "You are one. You charge 520
percent a year interest, compounded, on a simple loan.
According to my father's law books, that's a loan
shark."

"Since when did you start reading law books?" First
Mate retorted.

"Since I started doing research for you . . . duh!" Billy
replied.

First Mate relaxed a bit. "Oh, that's right, but I never
asked you to look up loan-sharking."

"No, Tad did, so we could figure out how to help you," Billy replied.

"Tell him that you're sorry. Tell him. You are a loan shark, whether you like the idea or not," Tad said.

Billy moved toward the desk.

First Mate looked at Angel. "Are you against me, too?"

"None of us are, but the law is the law, and Billy and Tad are right," Angel said quietly. "You can't charge 520 percent interest a year."

"That's what the market pays!" First Mate protested.

Tad settled the matter. He'd picked up a lot about banking at home, mostly by osmosis.

"It's a federal crime to charge more interest than the Federal Banking Commission allows. You're breaking the law and that's that," he told First Mate.

"So what are they going to do . . . put me in jail?" First Mate sulked.

"That's what we're trying to figure out," Angel sighed, handing Cappy to First Mate. She looked as if she needed him.

Billy took a seat at the desk. "You could go to Leavenworth. Did you ever hear of it? It's a federal prison."

"Don't be snotty," Angel told him.

"I'm not. I'm being honest," he replied. "Maybe I should have made a printout of what my father's law book says, so you'd believe me."

Tad pulled on his bushy hair. "I don't think they'd send a kid to Leavenworth," he told Billy.

"You know as well as I do that a person could commit murder and not be in as much trouble as a person who plays around with the U.S. banking laws," he replied.

First Mate did have one thing going for her. As far as Billy could figure, there weren't any laws about juvenile loan sharks. On the other hand, there wasn't anything in the racketeering laws about how old one had to be.

"Couldn't your father have rented Jessica's place to somebody else?" Tad asked.

"My father? He doesn't have anything to do with Jessica's house. It's that goon Charlie. He owns it. He owns my father's business. He . . . he. . . ."

First Mate caught herself too late. She'd let the secret out of the bag. The words spilled so easily. She felt like a dog. How could she have done that? If her parents ever found out. . . . Her hands began to tremble.

Tad played with the pile of the rug. Billy got up and walked to the window. Angel picked Cappy from the floor and handed him to First Mate. She looked as though she needed him again.

"You didn't hear what I just didn't say," First Mate told them, but it was too late. She couldn't say that she hadn't said what everybody had clearly heard her say. She couldn't put the words back in her throat. They were out, and once words are let out, they can't be caught and put back.

"I should have guessed that something obnoxious was in the air," she murmured, playing with Cappy's foot. "Tonight outside Sam's and then at the Station everybody looked at me like I was a piranha."

She held Cappy close to her heart, but that didn't help the knot in her stomach. Suddenly, she felt light-headed. The room began to spin. Lights floated in front of her eyes. She closed them, but the lights didn't go away. She lay back on her pillow.

Angel was first to notice that something was wrong.

"Are you okay?" she asked.

The voice stretched like an earthworm's body from one end of a tunnel to the other, growing thinner and deeper as it traveled.

Angel put her hand on First Mate's head. It was clammy.

"Billy?"

He turned from the window.

"Get that pillow out from under her head. Get it down. Get her feet up. You've got to get the blood flowing back to the head," Billy said, pulling the bottom of First Mate's sheet free. He grabbed her legs.

Angel handed him a pillow. Tad grabbed the others from the floor. He and Angel moved First Mate, until they got her head down off the side of the bed. Her eyes were still shut tightly.

Grams stood behind Billy. She looked just like her picture in the living room, except she was white, everything white, even her hair. Her dress was white, her skin opaque, her clothes the color of milk, her eyes glittered like diamonds.

Grams watched Billy massage First Mate's feet. She nodded in approval, then smiled at First Mate. Such a beautiful, happy smile.

"What are you so happy about?" First Mate asked.

Grams disappeared.

Tad returned with a glass of water. He held First Mate's head up, so she could drink it. She opened her eyes. Billy was still rubbing her feet. Angel placed the wet towel Tad had brought on her head. The floating lights disappeared.

First Mate took a sip and pushed the glass away.

"I'm losing it. My dead grandmother was just standing behind you, Billy."

"Oh, that's wonderful. Now I know everything will be all right," Angel exclaimed.

Billy rolled his eyes. Tad grinned, but Angel kept right on talking.

"Remember that time Billy and I got buried in the cave-in? I never told anybody but I saw my mother then. She was so beautiful. I knew as soon as I saw her that somebody would find us."

"What color were her eyes?" First Mate asked.

"They weren't any color. They glittered, sort of like diamonds. She was very clear, but she was all . . . like a white light. Is that what your grandma looked like?"

First Mate took another sip of water. Tad put the glass on the night table and propped up the pillows behind her.

"Is it?" Angel asked.

First Mate closed her eyes again, but Grams didn't reappear, so she opened them.

"Yes. She glittered."

18

All the kids but PJ were sound asleep in Mr. and Mrs. Tate's bed. Angel wanted to put them in their own beds, but Billy said to leave them alone. First Mate's parents could take care of them when they got home.

PJ came upstairs to the attic looking like the sawdust man. He'd cut out four birdhouses and sanded the wood.

First Mate was lying back on the pillows feeling sorry for herself. Tate Bank was doing so well. Business couldn't be better. She'd just hired Billy to help make collections, and now she had to chuck the whole thing —either that or go to jail. Damn Daddy! She hated him.

"My sister okay?" PJ asked, looking at First Mate.

It wasn't like her to be in bed before he was.

"I'm fine, PJ," First Mate smiled, opening her eyes.

"So how come you look like hell?" he asked.

Billy couldn't help but snicker. PJ was starting to sound like his sister.

"Move," Angel glared.

"What's your problem?" Billy asked.

"I need paper."

Billy was sitting at the desk.

"She's just tired. That's all, PJ," Angel explained, rummaging through a drawer. "We're going to let her sleep late tomorrow morning. We'll deliver the newspapers."

Billy and Tad looked at one another like, uh—does that include us? However, they didn't say anything, not until they were sure. Angel brought a pad and pencil to First Mate.

"Do you think you're up to drawing us a map of your paper route?" she asked.

"What for?" First Mate asked.

"I just said what for. Billy, Tad, and I are going to deliver the papers tomorrow morning. You're going to sleep late, for a change."

"That's news to—"

Tad had wanted to finish with the word "us," as in "That's news to us," but Angel glared him down. He shrugged. Oh well. Maybe he should help First Mate out. It was the least he could do to make up for thinking her father was a loan shark.

"Believe me. You don't want to do my papers," First Mate told Angel. You have to get up before the sea gulls. It's freezing cold out. And it takes forever. Besides, you wouldn't be able to handle my bike. Nobody can but I."

"Uh . . . I think that's 'but me,'" Angel smirked. "'Me' is the objective pronoun, object of the preposition 'but.'"

First Mate was too miserable to notice Angel's feeble attempt to get her to smile. "How much?" she asked.

"How much what?" Angel returned.

"How much do you want me to pay you?"

"Who said anything about payment? We're doing this for free. Right, guys?" Angel said.

"Well, I can't let you. I just can't. It's too much of a job," First Mate sighed.

Billy and Tad were relieved too soon, for Angel was not about to give up. She'd never delivered newspapers. It wasn't a world tour, but it was something different to do on a Sunday morning. Besides, it was only *one* morning. It wouldn't kill them, and Miss Sally would drive them around, so First Mate didn't have to worry about her bicycle. It just might be fun, and then they'd all go for breakfast later on at Angel's house.

"Me too?" PJ asked.

"If you help us."

He was in.

"That's awful! You're going to breakfast without me," First Mate complained. "All these years I've been delivering papers, and you never helped, and now you decide to deliver just one morning, and you make a circus out of it, and you don't even invite me. You leave me here! You say I can sleep, but I'll have to get up to mind the kids, anyway."

"Are you for real?" Angel asked her.

"I don't know. I just don't know."

First Mate arranged the pillows and curled under her quilt. Her world was smashed into so many splinters that she couldn't begin to glue them back together. She wished everybody would go away. Angel, Billy, Tad, PJ . . . just go away and let her sleep.

PJ took Angel's arm. "She keeps her customer list on the shelf in the front hall. I think there's a map, too. She made one just in case she ever got sick."

First Mate was sound asleep. PJ turned out the light and they all tiptoed downstairs. He found the customer list and then went up to take his shower (in Grams's room, of course). There wasn't any map, but he knew where everybody lived.

Angel and the boys went to the kitchen. It was eerie to sit at First Mate's table without First Mate. It was stranger, too, to know her parents weren't home, and all those kids were upstairs.

Angel went to the phone and dialed Miss Sally.

Could she sleep at First Mate's house, tonight?

Of course her parents were home! Whatever made Miss Sally think they weren't?

Oh, and would Miss Sally pick up Billy and Tad at 5 A.M. and bring them over here, so everybody could deliver First Mate's newspapers? They were going to make a party out of it, and then have breakfast back at—

Oh, and did Miss Sally mind making breakfast for about nine people tomorrow? Not too early—right after they finished delivering the newspapers.

It would have worked. It could have worked. It should have worked. That is, Miss Sally might have been fooled if Elizabeth hadn't run sobbing into the room.

"Where's my sister?"

"Shhhh," Billy said.

"I want my sister!"

"You can't have her. She's asleep," Tad said.

"I need my sister!"

Angel dropped the receiver to catch Elizabeth on her way up the stairs.

"Let me go! I want my sister," she sobbed.

19

*"L*izzie, whizzie peed the bed.
She peed so bad her rear turned red."

Barry sang at the top of his lungs. Ferdy and Christopher laughed so hard they couldn't stand up, so they sat on the shower floor and laughed some more. Miss Sally had a fit.

"You keep that up, Barry, and I'll wrap you in a towel and send you down the laundry chute," she warned.

Barry wasn't sure whether or not Miss Sally would actually do that. First Mate had once, when he was smaller. He'd landed on top of all the dirty sheets. It was fun. This time, though, he'd land on the floor. The dirty clothes were all washed. Barry shut up.

"It's not the end of the world, honey. You just think it is," Miss Sally soothed, as she wrapped Elizabeth in her father's enormous bath towel.

"Why don't you drop my brothers out the window?" Elizabeth wailed.

"I can't do that," Miss Sally said, opening Mrs. Tate's after-bath lotion.

"Then I'm gonna tell Daddy to when he comes home," Elizabeth declared.

"Fine," Miss Sally agreed, innocently, as she rubbed

the soothing lotion on Elizabeth's back. "Now put on your nightie and we're off to the kitchen. If those boys tease you tomorrow, drown them in the toilet."

Elizabeth liked that.

Angel's palaver over the phone hadn't fooled Miss Sally a bit. She knew darn well that First Mate's parents were nowhere near that house, and therefore was at First Mate's back door two minutes after she hung up on Angel.

By then the place was in an uproar. Elizabeth bawled because Angel wouldn't let her wake up First Mate. Christopher, Barry, and Ferdy yowled because Elizabeth soaked them. PJ bellowed for everybody to "*Shut Up.*"

The only two quiet people were Tad and Billy, and that was because they were flabbergasted.

Miss Sally rescued Elizabeth from Angel and carried her up to her parents' bathroom. On the way, she instructed Billy and Tad to "tackle those three monkeys and dump them in the shower." She told PJ to find some clean pajamas for his brothers and sister, and instructed Angel to make lots of toast and heat some milk.

How First Mate slept though the commotion was a mystery. Maybe her dream told her that someone was around to take over. Maybe she was so totally worn out that the house could have blown into the Atlantic Ocean, and she wouldn't have opened an eye until it bumped into England. Whatever the reason, she was out!

Angel found bread in the freezer, but had no luck locating milk. She sent Billy and Tad to 7–11 for a gallon . . . or two . . . whatever the three dollars she gave them covered. In the meantime, she toasted lots of bread and slathered it with honey, which was all she could find. However, she couldn't find any dishes.

"No dishes," Elizabeth said. "Mommy has to buy a new set."

She got the paper stuff from the pantry.

Billy and Tad returned with milk at about the same time that Miss Sally bribed Ferdy, Christopher, and Barry "to leave Elizabeth alone. In short, don't tease her. Don't needle her. Don't mock her." She promised pancakes for breakfast—at her house!

"Apple pancakes?" asked Barry.

"What a good idea," Miss Sally said.

"*OKAY!*"

"Ok-k-k-kay!"

"Okay!"

They all went downstairs for honey toast and warm milk. True to his promise, Barry, the ringleader, didn't say a word about Elizabeth drinking milk before bed. He didn't even "innocently" inform Miss Sally that First Mate never let his sister have anything to drink before bed. He was very proud of himself.

Tad poured the milk. He thought it was fun, kind of like a boarding school with so many kids sitting at the counter.

"You don't have a clue what boarding school is all about," Angel scowled.

She'd been to boarding school once. It was the absolute pits. There was a poltergeist and. . . .

"Nevermind! We've had enough lies for one night," Miss Sally said, sharply.

"Well, I knew you wouldn't let me stay overnight if I told you—"

"Shhhh!" Miss Sally cut in.

Billy and Tad made a fast exit. They promised to be on First Mate's front porch at five in the morning.

"You gonna stay over with Angel?" PJ asked Miss Sally.

"I'm going to stay with you all until your parents get home," she replied.

PJ went upstairs and returned with his grandmother's quilt and pillows.

"The couch in the den is the best. Better get some sleep. We have to get up awful early," he told Miss Sally.

After PJ left, Angel asked the obvious.

"Do you really think Mr. and Mrs. Tate will stay out all night?"

"I don't know what to think" Miss Sally frowned.

Angel was exhausted. She dragged herself up to the attic, where First Mate snored away. She didn't miss a snuzzle as Angel crawled into bed. Angel fell asleep making believe the snores were the whistles of the Siberian Railroad. She and her father chugged across Russia together.

The radio alarm blasted her out of bed.

Darn! She couldn't figure out how to turn it off. First Mate got up, walked around the bed, turned off the alarm, walked back to her side of the bed, and crawled in. Angel groped for the lamp and clicked it on. She found her clothes and clicked it off.

It was pitch dark. Not even the shadows were up yet. They had more sense.

I must have been crazy to offer to do this, Angel thought, as she groped across the room to the stairs. First Mate got up, walked past Angel, and turned on the stairway light.

"There's a switch at the bottom," she mumbled, and trudged back to bed. She turned off her second alarm clock and snuggled in.

By the time Angel reached the second floor switch, First Mate was again snoring peacefully.

The hall was not so dark. Nightlights offered enough light for Angel to hurry along. Mr. and Mrs. Tate's bedroom door was open. Angel couldn't help but notice that their bed was empty.

Downstairs, Angel found Miss Sally asleep in the den. She tiptoed past to the kitchen, where she put on her clothes. She went to the foyer and turned on the porch light. Then she took the knife and bags from the closet and laid them on the floor. PJ arrived on tiptoes.

"How'd you wake up?" Angel murmured.

"I don't know. I just did," he whispered.

They watched for Billy and Tad from the living room window.

The house was deadly silent. Not even the walls creaked. There was no trusty tick-tock of a grandfather clock. There was no friendly swish of trees against a familiar window. Angel felt like a fish out of water.

At last, Billy and Tad arrived. PJ let them in.

"It's freezing out," Tad blustered.

"Shhh! Miss Sally's still asleep," Angel whispered, shutting the door.

"She's here?" Billy asked.

"In the den," Angel murmured.

Billy was about to ask why, when PJ asked him for a hand with the bundle of newspapers he was so bravely trying to drag inside. Billy helped him. Tad followed with another bundle. Billy and Tad hauled in two more, and Angel cut off the plastic bindings. PJ tried to tow in the pack of ads and extras that are part and parcel of anybody's Sunday newspaper, but again the task was hopeless. Tad rescued him.

Somehow, the four of them managed to put together all 125 Sunday editions. First Mate would have had a fit if she'd seen the way they did it, but Angel, Billy, Tad, and PJ were pleased.

Time to awaken Miss Sally. Obviously, the turmoil in the foyer hadn't bothered her a bit.

"Wha? . . . What? . . ."

Miss Sally was discombobulated. She sat up and looked around.

"They're not home *yet?*" she asked Angel, then put her finger to her lips. *Hush!*

PJ stood behind Angel.

"Where did you park your car? We can't find it,"

"Of course you can't," Miss Sally declared, dragging

herself off the couch. "I didn't drive. I ran!"

Angel walked her back to the house. Rather, they ran back because they were very late. First Mate told them to deliver the papers by 7 A.M. It was already 7:15, and they hadn't even started.

Miss Sally needed a good run. She wanted to lambaste First Mate's parents, but since they weren't around, she'd have sailed into Angel—Angel needed a good blasting for telling her that Ellie and Pete Tate were home last night—but this wasn't the time and place for it. She'd fix Angel's wagon in private.

They returned in the Land Rover. PJ showed the boys how First Mate's trestle worked, and in no time at all the canvas bags were rolled into the car.

Angel barked the directions PJ had written. He, Billy and Tad ran from house to house. The sun climbed higher above the shroud of clouds. At the Tate house, First Mate and the little ones slept like kittens.

Mr. and Mrs. Tate were also asleep in the king-size bed of a luxury suite at Diamond Lil's in Atlantic City. They were guests of the management (so they thought). Mr. Tate's dreams were in stacks of 5-thousand-dollar chips, piled on the deck of the yacht he'd sold to pay off markers. Mrs. Tate's dreams jingled with coins cascading into a colossal bucket that grew like Jack's beanstalk to the sky.

Miss Sally turned the Land Rover into the Tate driveway.

"Give me an hour," she told Angel.

20

Miss Sally was in seventh heaven. Kids filled her big kitchen to the brim, Angel, First Mate, Billy, Tad, PJ, Ferdy, Barry, Christopher, and Elizabeth. Wall to wall children gobbled up apple pancakes as fast as she could flip them. She cored another apple and put it in the peeler. She pulled the peeled apple from the peeler and put it in the slicer. She pulled the sliced apple from the slicer and stirred it into the new batch of batter. She poured the batter on the super-size griddle. On both sides, the pancakes were smooth as velvet and brown as toast. Miss Sally was delighted.

First Mate sat at the head of the table. Angel and Tad were on either side of her. Billy sat next to Angel and PJ across from him. And so it went down the line with the rest of the gang seated according to age.

Miss Sally declared that First Mate was neither to pour juice nor slice a flapjack. She was not to worry whether the kids ate or didn't eat, whether they argued or didn't argue, whether they spilled juice or didn't. Angel, Billy, and Tad would take care of those little tasks. PJ could help, if he chose. Naturally, he chose, so First Mate didn't know what to do with herself.

"Have another pancake," Miss Sally suggested, flipping two hot ones on her plate.

"That's not fair. She got three, already. I only got one," Barry complained.

"Shut up, Barry. We won't get invited back," Ferdie said, but nobody heard him. On the other hand, nobody paid attention to Barry either.

First Mate sprinkled cinnamon over the butter melting on her hotcakes. It was Miss Sally's idea. Slosh the cinnamon in with the butter then pour on the maple syrup. Cinnamon, maple syrup, and butter work best with apples. First Mate sliced the round, flat cakes into neat cubes. She popped in the first mouthful.

"Hmmm," she nodded, but Miss Sally was already back at the apple slicer.

"C-c-c-c-can I h-h-h-have m-m-m-m-more?" Christopher asked her.

Miss Sally hadn't noticed him get up from the table. He was pale and thin, very much like First Mate. His hair hung in draggles over his forehead.

"P-p-p-p-please, M-m-m-miss Sally, c-c-c-c-can I h-h-h-h-have m-m-m-more?"

"Of course you can," Miss Sally trilled.

She slipped two pancakes from the griddle to his plate.

"T-t-t-t-t-h-hanks," he grinned.

Miss Sally watched Christopher carry his plate to the table, then turned to her griddle.

"I suppose his parents have more important things

than his stuttering on their minds," she grumbled.

At that moment in the Diamond Lil Casino, Mr. and Mrs. Tate were so busy trying to hit the jackpot that neither remembered the other existed, nevermind both should remember their son Christopher had a bad stutter.

Mom was lost in the "Jacks or Higher" slots. She sat stiff as a poker watching the word PLAY chase itself in blinking letters across the screen. The machine was getting cold. It had started out hot enough. An hour ago, she was winning hand over fist. The electronic calliope inside the glass box sang the winner tune so many times that anyone would have thought it was set on rerun. The credits grew higher each time she hit BET MAX.

Once, just for the fun of hearing her winnings jingle, Mom had cashed out. The calliope sang its song. Bells rang, and a windfall of coins chimed down to the tray. She filled the bucket. Now, it was nearly empty. Ellie Tate wondered if she should try a new machine.

For the first time all morning, she looked around. Strangers filled every seat in sight. Coins jingled into machines. Calliopes played. Coins jangled into waiting trays.

A waitress passed. Ellie signaled her.

"Orange juice."

She and Daddy hadn't bothered with breakfast. That might be the problem. Her sugar was low. The machine could have sensed it and gone to sleep.

Ellie noticed a young couple standing near the arch. They watched her intently. Ellie smiled, and they returned the greeting. They wanted her machine.

The waitress brought the orange juice. Ellie slipped her a fat tip.

"What do you think about this spot?" Ellie asked.

"Like I told you before. The jackpot's overdue," the waitress replied. "You just have to keep playing, keep playing. Somebody's got to win."

The Diamond Lil didn't have too many "Progressive Jacks High" slots—and now that the jackpot was up to $110 thousand—.

The winning hand was a royal heart flush. Ellie had hit one two years before. That was when she'd first started driving down with Pete. She didn't have a clue what she was doing. She had put her coin in the slot and, "blip, blip, blip, blip, blip," she had a ten, jack, queen, and king, of hearts. She wouldn't have guessed that she was such a winner except the bell went off. Two hundred fifty dollars just like that. It could have been a million, she was so excited.

Well, this time I'm going to win *big* money, and won't Pete drop his teeth?

Ellie pictured her husband's face when she showed him that certified check for $110 thousand. That would be a reckoning. A thrill fluttered around her heart.

"The way he puts down my slots . . . like his craps are so much better," she murmured to herself.

Her hands were clammy. She pointed to BET MAX, then pulled her finger away. Maybe she shouldn't. Suppose she lost? She didn't have much money left.

Well, *she'd better win it all back and then plenty more!*

On the other side of the room, Daddy had already built his winnings to an awesome amount. The craps table was hot. He'd bet right all morning. He and his cronies were having a blast.

A stranger picked his dice. He looked tense.

No good, Pete thought.

He signaled the dealer to take his odds down, then put $1000 on "Don't Pass."

Sure enough. Snake eyes.

"I should have bet *ten thousand*," Pete grumbled, as he quickly signaled the dealer to add that much to the next bet.

"Sorry, I've got to go wrong on this one," he told his buddies.

Nobody had time to follow him. They lost. Pete won.

Someone slapped him on the back.

"Damn! That's good!"

"And he's going to roll it again," Pete said, signaling the dealer.

The dice hit the side of the table, rolled to the middle, and fell still.

"Snake eyes again!" the dealer called.

Pete's heart pounded stronger than the surf outside the casino. His ears echoed the sound. His hands trembled.

"I have to keep cool. Have to keep cool. I'm going to win back every dollar I ever lost. Thursday was just for practice."

Pete's brain was charged. He had five, then six, then seven bets going at once. Four, five, six, ten, give odds, don't come, don't pass. He followed the shooter bet for bet. The piles of chips multiplied.

Cash in and get out of here, a little voice told him. Forget that.

Wherever the shooter's chips moved, Pete's followed.

Cash in and get out of here, the voice repeated.

Pete signaled half his winnings off the table. They were by then $100 thousand. Imagine! Half his winnings were a hundred thousand dollars!

The shooter crapped out!

Pete watched the dealer rake away his bets. Two new dealers joined the game. The dealer handed one of them the rake. The other placed bets where the players directed. The new shooter picked his dice. Pete wiped the sweat dripping into his eyes.

The shooter rolled. The dice hit the side of the table and bounced to the middle. Pete's bet won!

I'll win back that hundred thousand and then some, he thought.

His hands trembled so badly that he had to signal the dealer to place his next bets.

Outside the casino, an introductory dusting of snow exploded to the blizzard that had already hit Shadow Lawn.

21

"**O**h my!"

Miss Sally dropped the apple and stared out the window.

"That's some storm!"

"Oh my . . . Angel! . . . the horses. . . ."

Nine children at a table, and who's to hear Miss Sally say something about a horse, with so much chatter and silverware clinking against plates? No notice of the nor'easter that's rolled in like a tidal wave.

"I knew I shouldn't have put those horses out. I said to myself, 'Don't do it, Sally,' but I did."

Miss Sally had put the horses in the corral when she returned from driving the kids around town with the newspapers. Something told her to do that; then she remembered she was fuming at Angel, so she decided not to; but she was already on her way to the barn, so she kept going. It wasn't Sasha's and Pasha's fault that Angel'd lied. They were used to exercise early in the morning. It wasn't the Tate kids' fault either. They deserved a decent breakfast of a Sunday morning.

"Angel!" Miss Sally called.

"When did the snow start? I don't know. I was so busy."

"*Angel!*"

Everybody heard that and looked up and gasped and raced to the window.

"I can't see!" Elizabeth yelled.

Miss Sally picked Elizabeth up and gave her to Billy.

"What do I do with her?" he asked.

"Put her on your shoulders," Miss Sally replied, reaching for Christopher. "Tad, help me here."

They set Christopher and Barry in the double sink. That made Ferdy so angry that he actually yelled loud enough for attention. Miss Sally had Tad put him on the counter next to the sink. Ten sets of disbelieving eyes gawked out the window.

This was not the usual Shadow Lawn plop, fizz, rained-out-before-a-kid-could-drag-the-sled-from-under-the-beach-umbrella snow. This was the real McCoy—the great white shark!

Good snow! Thick snow! Worthy snow! Marvelous snow! Glorious snow! No school for at least a week snow!

This was a moment set by the heavens to thank the Lord of the Snows for such a fine gift. Not a word was said aloud. Not even a breath could be heard until Barry let out a whoop that sliced the silence like a buzz saw on carrot cake.

"Quiet!" First Mate scolded.

She shouldn't have wasted her breath. The spell was broken. Barry's whoop did it.

PJ took up the cheer.

"Hoorah!"

Elizabeth followed.

"*Yippee!*"

Ferdy came next.

"*Yeow!*"

Christopher didn't even stutter.

"*It's snowing good!*"

"Well," First Mate corrected, pushing in between Tad and Billy. "It's snowing well."

"Well" wasn't as good as "good." "Well" stunk. Besides, Christopher had uttered three whole words without a stutter!

First Mate didn't care. How would her parents ever get home?

"You'd better get those horses in," Miss Sally reminded Angel.

"I wish you hadn't put them out," Angel groused.

"I wish I hadn't either, but I did, so that's that," Miss Sally said.

"I'll go with you," First Mate volunteered.

She couldn't just stand there. She was too nervous. Besides—her stomach hurt.

Miss Sally began immediately with orders on what Angel should put on, and what she should lend First Mate to keep warm and dry. Angel closed her ears, rolled her eyes, and got First Mate out of the kitchen fast.

"She's such a pest."

"I wouldn't mind being pestered like that once in a while," First Mate frowned. Angel was already choosing the coats, gloves, and boots for the trek to the corral.

"Here. Try these."

Angel handed First Mate a pair of deerskin boots. They were hand-made by Hopi Indians and lined with fur softer than Elizabeth's curls.

"Are you kidding? You don't *wear* these. You hang them over the mantle," First Mate told Angel.

"We'll do that later. Put them on your feet for now."

"No way."

First Mate pulled her skullcap over her ears and followed Angel to the back porch. Neither of the girls had any idea what to expect, for the screening was plugged with snow, so they didn't realize that the wind was so strong—that is, until Angel opened the door and nearly blew away with it. She let go mighty fast.

"We need scarves," she told First Mate.

They returned to the mudroom. This time First Mate gladly pulled on those fancy warm boots and a Siberian parka and a long English muffler that wound around her face and tied behind the parka hood—and thick suede mittens.

Again they faced the wind, which buffeted them like paper dolls from one side of the driveway to the other until they got enough sense to link arms and move to the protection of the trees. Snow bit their eyes and iced their eyebrows. Warm breath froze on their scarves.

They stopped at the barn for a breather. Angel slid open the door and they slipped inside to peel the scarves from their mouths.

"This has to be worse than Siberia," Angel remarked.

First Mate retied her muffler and headed out. She didn't want to think about how bad *this* was. She didn't want to think about anything, especially her parents. Were they still in the casinos? *Were they on their way home? Were they stalled somewhere on the parkway? Would they run out of gas? Would they freeze to death before a trooper found them?*

The open field was the worst. With no trees or bushes to protect them, the girls had to crawl like six-legged turtles toward the corral. Visibility was nil, but they managed at last to bump into the fence.

Angel pulled the muffler down and let out a whistle. The horses returned with angry neighs.

"Aw shut up and get over here," First Mate muttered.

She vaguely saw their silhouettes trotting around the corral. Once, they came so near she could almost touch them.

Angel whistled again. The horses whinnied their reply. First Mate decided that three little brothers were not so bad. At least they had enough sense to come in from the cold.

Angel whistled again. This time Sasha and Pasha turned and headed toward the sound.

Angel put a set of reins in First Mate's hand.

"Grab the mane," she shouted.

Pasha, whose reins First Mate held, sensed what to do. He moved closer to First Mate and waited until she gained enough courage to let go of the fence and grab his mane. Then he moved near the fence, so she could use it to boost herself on to his back. She slumped low and held tight.

First Mate buried her face in Pasha's mane, letting him take charge of the walk to the barn. His easy stride was comforting. His soft mane warmed her face.

At the barn, the horses knew exactly what to do. They shielded Angel from the wind while she dismounted and opened the door. They waited for her to turn on the light before they entered.

First Mate dismounted. Pasha clopped into his stall. Angel and First Mate slid the barn door shut and dropped to the floor in exhaustion. The mufflers defrosted, and they pulled them from their mouths.

"Why don't we wrap up in some blankets and take a nap?" First Mate sighed.

"We can't. We've got to rub down the horses. They might catch cold," Angel said, jumping up.

She took liniment from the shelf. "Here. This is good for you, too. Rub it on your hands. They'll feel wonderful."

Angel was right. First Mate's rough hands began to feel delicious. Soon she was rubbing Pasha's coat with the soothing liniment. Then she brushed him and gave him some carrots and a little sugar. She and Angel moved the horses into clean stalls. They shoveled out the dirty ones. As Angel put the manure buckets outside, the blast of frigid air reminded the girls that they still had a miserable hike to the house.

"We could always take the sleigh" she grinned, sliding the door shut.

In the open space on the other side of the barn was the sleigh Angel's father had sent with Sasha and Pasha from Siberia. It was a relic of long ago when people in Russia rode in sleighs pulled by three horses.

"It's called a *troika*," Angel said, climbing into the driver's seat.

First Mate climbed next to her.

"Usually my father doesn't do anything with old stuff. He says that once it's changed or even fixed up, it loses its value. But he had this *troika* all redone for me. See? Two horses can pull it now."

On the back seat lay a fur comforter. First Mate cozied herself under it.

"Get up! Don't you dare fall asleep! We've got to get back to the house before Miss Sally sends for the Marines," Angel commanded.

She pulled the comforter off First Mate.

"Damn!"

First Mate climbed over the back of the carriage and jumped down. As she landed, her hand touched a brass engraving. In square letters was the name Angelica. The brass seemed very new—at least it was shined and lacquered to look like new.

"That's a funny name for a sleigh," she said, running her fingers over the word.

Angel rolled her eyes. She always did when something bothered her.

"So what's the problem?" First Mate asked.

"No problem."

Angel climbed under the comforter that First Mate had just abandoned.

"Hey! Get up. If I can't sleep then neither can you."

"I'm not sleeping. I'm hiding. Go away!"

First Mate reached into the carriage and grabbed the comforter, but Angel had wrapped herself so tightly that First Mate couldn't get a good grip.

"Damn! What's your problem?"

As First Mate pulled away, her hand again touched the brass plate. Suddenly, she knew.

"Oh my! I can't believe it!"

She giggled.

"Don't you tell a soul!" Angel warned from beneath the blanket.

"Your name is Angelica? A-N-G-E-L-I-C-A!"

Only First Mate, Miss Emily Tate, could have guessed so easily. A broad smile sneaked across her face. She wasn't the only person in the world who had a name to hide. Angel—Angelica—of course! It made sense!

"A bit hoity-toity . . . don't you think?" First Mate teased.

Angel peeked from under the blanket.

"My father tells me that my mother did it," she sighed, rolling her eyes again.

"Of course he does. Your poor mother's dead. She can't stick up for herself," First Mate replied.

"Oooh. This is terrible. I think I'd like to die myself," Angel sighed.

Suddenly, First Mate felt sorry. The guilt pinched her

toes and turned her stomach again. What an awful thing to say to her best friend—*Sure, your mother's dead!*

Angel threw off the blanket and knelt on the *troika's* back seat.

"Can you imagine? What were my parents thinking?" she asked First Mate.

The knot in First Mate's stomach grew tighter.

"Angelica has a nice ring to it," she said. "Really it does."

She hoped saying such a kind thing would untie her stomach, but it didn't. The pain grew worse. First Mate knew without a doubt that there was only one thing she could do to save her almighty soul (and sad stomach) from misery for being so mean to her dearest friend. She reached up and jingled the brass bells strung above the nameplate.

"Angelica," she sang.

"Give it up," Angel groused.

First Mate jingled the bells again.

"Angelica, Angelica, I have something to tellica," she sang.

The bells had a happy ring, like Christmas, but Angel couldn't smile.

"Help?" First Mate asked.

Usually she was great at making up ditties, but not just then.

"Please?" she asked Angel.

"Tell me what you willica," Angel grumbled.

"I can't. It doesn't rhymica," First Mate sang, help-lessly. "Help me outica."

"Change the rhyme pattern," Angel told her.

"Good idea. Now let me see. Oh yes," She jingled the bells again.

"You see . . ."

Jingle.

"Dear me . . ."

Jingle.

"Really . . ."

Jingle.

"I am . . ."

Triple jingle.

"An *Emily*!"

First Mate let go of the bells, grabbed the blanket, pulled it from Angel, wrapped herself in it, and sat on the floor. Angel, kneeling on the back seat, peered down, nonplussed.

First Mate's stomach felt a bit better. She stood up and offered Angel her hand.

"Angelica Wilson, meet Emily Tate."

First Mate dropped the quilt.

"*Emily?*" Angel repeated.

"Emily," First Mate grinned.

"Emily," Angel said again, rolling the name around her tongue. "You're really an Emily? You're not just making this up to make me feel better?"

"My parents were very young. They didn't know any

better," First Mate sighed. "Are you going to shake my hand or what, because my arm's getting tired."

"Emily?" Angel asked again, incredulously.

First Mate gave up and dropped her hand. This was so embarrassing. On the other hand, her stomach felt better.

Angel sat down. Emily! Where did such a name come from?

An Emily was definitely not a First Mate. An Emily was a fancy girl. She'd wear fussy clothes. She'd probably curl her hair, or if it were straight, she'd let it grow long so it hung like silk on her back. An Emily was dainty. She didn't say, "damn" or "hell" or "aw shut up!"

Angel turned around and knelt again on the seat, peering down at First Mate, who at that moment wore such a ridiculous, pained, embarrassed, chagrined look that Angel burst out laughing.

"I'm trying to be nice!" First Mate cried.

"It's hil-ar-eeee-us!" Angel managed to sputter between bursts of laughter.

"No worse than *Angelica*," First Mate pouted, but Angel was too busy laughing to hear.

Laughter is more contagious than the best winter flu, and not even First Mate could defend herself against it. Pretty soon, her pout turned to a grin, then her grin to a giggle. She joined Angel in the *troika*, and the two of them let forth a battery of hees and haws and ha-ha-ha's until their ribs ached, but still they couldn't stop.

"Angelica!" First Mate hollered between bursts.

"Emily" Angel returned, flopping down on the seat.

First Mate reached back and jingled the *troika*'s bells, and they laughed some more. They laughed until they cried. They laughed until their ribs hurt so much they swore between whoops that they'd never laugh again. They laughed until the horses whinnied so loud that Angel remembered they needed to be fed. She sat up like a bolt of lightning.

"Oh my gosh! We'd better feed them and get going."

For whatever reason, the walk to the house was not as bad as the girls had expected it to be. Perhaps knowing that each of them had a true name she'd rather be without made it easier. Perhaps the blizzard had mellowed. Perhaps First Mate and Angel figured a way to let the hemlocks take the storm's punishment for them. They linked arms, lowered heads and plowed through the snow until their feet hit the invisible bottom step of the back porch.

They climbed up the steps. Angel groped until she found the door handle. One pull and the wind slammed the door backwards against the screening. The girls climbed inside.

"We're back!" Angel called from the mudroom.

Snow stuck to them like Miss Sally's sugar icing. They couldn't stomp it off.

"We're back!"

No answer.

Angel looked at First Mate. Where do you suppose they are?

The girls defrosted their scarves enough to remove

them, then headed for the warmth of the kitchen. It was empty. Miss Sally, the kids, even Billy and Tad had evaporated.

"Miss Sally?" Angel called, venturing into the hall.

A light flickered from the great front room. Angel and First Mate followed it. They found Miss Sally and the children cozily lodged in front of the blazing fire.

"Dick Wittington, twice Lord Mayor of London-town," Miss Sally read in sing-song from Angel's old book of fairy tales.

The kids, even PJ, were entranced.

"We're back," Angel announced.

"And freezing," First Mate added.

Miss Sally took one look at the two of them and let out a holler loud enough to send every mouse in the enormous old house scurrying.

"You're covered with snow!"

"We sure are. It's a monster out there."

"Well, don't just stand here melting all over the floor. You'll wreck it. Go on inside and get your coats off, and then go upstairs and take showers. You need hot showers. I'll fix you cocoa, but don't come back soon because I have to finish reading the kids this story."

"We saved the horses," First Mate said.

"We almost froze out there," Angel added.

"Out!" Miss Sally commanded. She returned to the fairy tale.

"Once upon a time there was a poor boy named, . . ."

22

The blizzard tapered off just before Barry, Ferdy, and Christopher awakened, which was at the crack of dawn. They'd slept together in the Wild West—each boy snugly clad in one of Dr. Wilson's old, long sleeved undershirts with the sleeves rolled up and pinned to stay put. The shirts themselves were longer than the boys so it took some doing for each to scramble to the window without falling on his face.

They watched day stumble in without a sun. Its gray light fell in shadows on the mounds of snow three floors below. Snow shrouded the barn. Beyond it, more snow buried the corral and the bushes that bordered the field. It covered the driveway that led to the barn.

"Wow!" Barry whispered.

The sight was truly awesome.

"W-w-we w-won't have school. That's f-f-f-er s-s-ure," Christopher said.

Ferdy didn't say a word. Nobody listened to him, anyway.

Across the hall and down three suites, First Mate tossed in her sleep. She'd picked the South Seas for a bedroom because it didn't snow ever in the South Pacific. It stayed warm all the time, so parents didn't get marooned in Atlantic City.

She'd called her house a hundred times that day but only gotten her mother's voice on the answer machine.

"Hi! It's Ellie Tate. You know the drill."

Maybe, there wasn't even an Atlantic City in the South Pacific. She didn't know. She dreamed of palm trees and flowers and a luau on the beach. It was great until a cold breeze swept in from the ocean. First Mate tucked her blanket around her.

Suddenly, she was cold. Ice cold on her face and her arms and neck. Barracudas had attacked from the ocean . . . freezing cold barracudas with ice for teeth!

First Mate's eyes opened. She sat up in bed!

"What are you doing here?"

No barracudas. Kids, yucky little brothers!

"Get outta here!"

"Gotcha!" Barry yelled.

"Yeah!" Ferdy hollered, pushing snow into her face. Christopher sloshed a big lump on her neck.

It dribbled down her spine.

"Monsters! You're monsters!" First Mate shrieked.

She might have called them hippogriffs, but she didn't think of the word. It was too early in the morning to do anything but jump out of bed and fight. Each time she hurled one brother out, the other two charged.

Finally, the miracle happened. They ran out of snow, and while they were rearming on the lanai outside First

Mate's sitting room, she slammed the door and ran for it.

She made for the suite with the French flag lowered outside. That would be where Angel was sleeping. First Mate let herself in with one hand and pulled down the flag with the other. Those hippogriffs *(she'd finally remembered the word)* shouldn't have a clue as to her whereabouts.

Angel was sound asleep in a high four-poster bed. Only her blond hair showed above the flowered quilt. First Mate tiptoed over and slipped into the bed. Mmmmm —so toasty—so cozy warm, but her feet were frozen. She moved to the middle and wrapped her icy feet around Angel's warm ones.

Angel pulled away. First Mate tried again. She'd never be able to sleep with such cold feet.

"Yeow!"

Angel jumped up in bed.

"What are you doing here?" she asked.

"Trying to get warm. The monsters attacked me," First Mate replied between chattering teeth.

"Can't you get warm somewhere else?" Angel asked.

"Not as fast as I can get warm here," First Mate said, snuggling into the warm pillow that Angel had just abandoned.

"I've got lots of beds. Try another," Angel suggested.

"You try," First Mate sighed, "and lock the door behind you because I don't want those kids attacking me again."

With that, she cozied in for good.

"Fine, I'll go sleep in Russia," Angel groused, but First Mate was already snoring.

Grams appeared.

"I'm on my way to the South Pacific," First Mate told her.

Grams wore a different outfit from the last dream, but she was still all white with beautiful opaque skin and dancing eyes.

"Good morning yourself," she told First Mate.

She sat in the chair near Angel's bed. Her aura glowed like the sun, so bright that First Mate had to cover her eyes. Grams gave her sunglasses.

"These will help."

"Those are Angel's. Where did you get them?"

"Put them on," said Grams.

First Mate put them on. Grams turned to yellow diamonds.

"You're looking good, Grams," she said, peering through the amber lenses.

"I'm looking well," Grams corrected.

She wasn't a ghost, not really, at least she didn't seem to be one. This time she wore her pink velvet dress, except it wasn't pink anymore. It was sparkling yellow.

"Is it possible that I'm dreaming?" First Mate asked her.

"You just told me that," Grams said.

"I did?"

"Yes. You asked me what I was doing in your dream."

"Oh," First Mate replied. "Well then. What are you doing in my dream?"

"I'm not," Grams told her.

"I'm confused," First Mate replied.

"Look around you," Grams directed.

"What at?" First Mate asked.

"Hush! You talk too much."

Angel's room had disappeared. They were outside flying—imagine that—flying in the cold wind, but First Mate wasn't a bit chilly, not even her feet. The gray clouds were gone and the sky was pink, like Grams's dress used to be. The snow on the ground beneath them was also pink, purple where the drifts were high.

"Nice," First Mate told Grams.

They passed the boat yard and headed up the river to the bay and then on over the Atlantic Ocean. The breakers were enormous, some as high as ocean liners.

"Cappy loves it out here. He swoops down when the wave is just cresting and slips right under the arc. Right before the wave breaks, he pops on up. He calls it hop-scotching. Imagine that . . . at his age playing hop-scotch."

"I don't see him," First Mate said, peering below.

"Of course you don't. That's because he isn't here. He's down Atlantic City way taking care of your parents. I gave up on those two. They're his job now."

First Mate felt herself dropping. Down. Down. Down. Nearer and nearer to the water. Another foot and she'd hit that swell waiting to form into a breaker. Down. Down. Down. Her heart spun. The swell became a breaker.

"Grams, help!"

"You're fine. Don't panic."

Gram's velvet voice was right above her.

First Mate tried to flap her arms, but they were too heavy.

Down. Down. Down.

"Grams!"

Her heart was in her throat. Blood rushed to her head. She'd fallen below the crest. Above was a giant pipeline waiting to swallow her.

"Grams!"

"I'm right here. It's okay! You're fine. Give me your hand!"

"I can't. I can't move!"

First Mate was paralyzed.

Gram's hands were on her shoulders, but it was too late! The wave broke!

First Mate wiped the water from her eyes. She was sitting up in bed. On the night table, an empty glass of water lay on its side.

Her heart still pounded. Her hands trembled, but she wasn't paralyzed anymore. She stood the glass upright. As she did, she noticed a pair of sunglasses resting near the lamp. Had they been there all along?

23

Barry was at it again, ringing that school bell until the dead couldn't sleep on Angel's third floor.

"Hear ye! Hear ye! Elizabeth didn't pee the bed!"

First Mate jumped out of bed and dashed down the hall and grabbed the gong—

"Hear yee. . . ."

Barry's voice trailed off, but he clung to the bell rope.

"Barry, you let go of that rope or I'll go down there and strangle you with it."

"Barry, let it go," Miss Sally warbled, emerging from the kitchen.

"Good afternoon," she called up to First Mate. "I sent Barry to wake you up. I should have guessed he'd go for that bell. He's been dying to ring it."

"Afternoon?" First Mate asked.

"We had lunch already," Barry called.

"Grilled cheese sandwiches," Elizabeth sang.

First Mate hadn't noticed her little sister follow Miss Sally from the kitchen.

"And guess what? I didn't pee last night. Miss Sally let me sleep near her, and I didn't pee!"

First Mate was nonplussed. Barry ringing the bell to

announce Elizabeth didn't wet the bed, and Elizabeth laughing about it? Her family was getting crazier by the minute.

"What time is it?" she asked, looking at her watch.

2:25 P.M.

"I never slept this late in my life!"

"Go on down to Russia. Angel left out warm clothes for you. As soon as she and PJ return with the kids' boots and such, we're going for a sleigh ride. They haven't cleaned the roads off yet, so we can go all over town. Are you hungry? I'll fix you eggs or cereal or grilled cheese—whatever you like," Miss Sally twittered in what seemed to be one continuous sentence.

"Did my mother call?" First Mate asked.

"Don't worry. It's best they stay wherever they are. Most of the highways are closed," Miss Sally piped.

"The telephones are out, too?" First Mate asked.

"Hurry. Get dressed. These kids are beside themselves to get in that Russian sled," Miss Sally sang. "What did you say you wanted for breakfast?"

Miss Sally'd ducked First Mate's questions. First Mate wanted to ask again, and again, and again if she had to. She wanted to scream it out louder than Barry rang the damn bell, but she knew she wouldn't get an answer. She ran back to French Country, jumped into bed, and covered her head with the pillow.

Where were they? Why didn't they call?

She'd totally forgotten about the newspapers she

hadn't delivered that morning. She didn't know that they were sitting back home on her front porch, and if she'd thought of it, she wouldn't have cared.

Why hadn't she brought Cappy with her? She always felt better when she could hug her Cappy.

Tears sprung from a place so deep in her heart she didn't know it existed. They burst like a breaker more powerful than any in her dreams. They smashed the barrier she'd so carefully built, day by day, week by week, year by year since Grams died. They wouldn't be held. They couldn't stop. If there is such a thing as crying one's heart out, First Mate did it.

Angel entered the room and sat by her bed. She tried to soothe her, but First Mate just sobbed, "Go 'way. Go 'way. Leave me alone!"

"I'll get Miss Sally," Angel said.

"No! I don't want her to see me like this. Just go away, please. Tell her I went back to sleep."

"I guess that means you don't want to ride with us," Angel said.

First Mate threw the pillow at her.

Even the greatest hurricane eventually wears itself out. So it was with First Mate. After a while, the tears ebbed, and the sobs grew more and more infrequent. She retrieved the pillow she'd hurled at Angel and lay back in bed hugging it. If her heart was still broken, she didn't know, for she felt totally numb.

Grams, help me. I don't know what to do, she thought.

Then she saw her. She closed her eyes and saw her grandmother's face, radiant, translucent, and glowing. She was above First Mate, looking down at her and *laughing*!

Laughing? How can you be laughing at a time like this? Mommy and Daddy are missing! They've flown the coop, or maybe they're dead somewhere in a big snowdrift, frozen cold! I want to call the police, but I'm scared. Suppose they're *not* dead? Suppose they're still in one of those awful casinos? Suppose they don't even know there's been a blizzard here?

Grams kept laughing, not making a sound, just grinning from ear to ear with such a heavenly glow that First Mate couldn't make head or tail of it. She finally decided that Grams was telling her not to worry.

Not to worry?

Not to worry. Everything would turn out okay.

Like the Cheshire cat in *Alice in Wonderland*, Grams disappeared. First Mate sat up. Her stomach didn't hurt anymore. Her head didn't even hurt, and she'd cried up a storm. Her pillow was all wet.

She went into the bathroom and threw cold water on her face. She didn't look too bad, considering. She doused a washcloth with more cold water and held it on her eyes. Soon the puffiness was down. She went inside and slipped on the woolen shirt and jeans that Angel had left out for her.

Downstairs was quiet as a church. The driveway was clear, but not salted. The marks from the sleigh ran up from the barn. Even Miss Sally'd gone for the ride. Good. First Mate had the house to herself.

She went to the phone and dialed home again.

"Hello?"

"*Mom?*"

"First Mate! Where are you?"

"Where am I? Where were you? I've been crazy worrying! You're all right?"

"Of course I'm all right."

"Daddy all right?"

"Well, he's on a bit of a tear. I'm afraid I'm going to have to go down with him again."

"Down where?"

As if First Mate didn't know.

"To Atlantic City. He lost big. He has to get the money back."

"With what?" First Mate asked.

Mom didn't answer that one.

"I have chicken soup in the cooker. It will be ready for supper. There are crackers in the pantry, and I bought a bag of apples. I thought I had cake mix. I was going to get a cake in before—"

Mom stopped short.

The seconds of dead air between Mom and First Mate seemed like hours. First Mate's senses went on alert. Her stomach tightened, but she didn't notice.

"Ma, where's Daddy getting the money to gamble some more?" she asked.

"Where are you?" Mom asked in return.

"I'm at Angel's. We're all here, at least we were here, but Angel and Miss Sally took the kids for a ride in the sleigh her father sent from Russia."

"If we're not back, will she let you stay the night?" Mom asked.

First Mate slammed down the phone.

Where was he getting more money? Where? There wasn't any in the house, not even the news paper money anymore. Mom said he was on a tear, but there wasn't any noise going on in the background. If he was on a tear, he'd be throwing things around and shouting and —

"Oh no!"

The thought was like winter lightning, fire and ice so sharp it nearly cut her in two. She sat down. She stood up. She grabbed the fur coat Angel had left out for her. She ran to the mudroom for those nice boots.

24

Angel'd practiced Sasha and Pasha pulling the *troika* in the field, and now they were off God knows where about town making every kid as jealous as a dragon. The field was empty. The snow in drifts higher than First Mate's waist, except for the undulating path Miss Angel had carved with Angelica. It ran in criss-crosses, circles, and ovals. First Mate hurried from one path to the other, taking the shortest route between Angel's yard and hers.

Maybe she was wrong. God, she hoped she was wrong. Please God, make her be wrong.

How could Daddy get inside Noah's Ark? The portal was double locked.

On the other hand, when Daddy had a crazy, he could do just about anything. He probably could smash those locks with his bare hands!

But he didn't know about Noah's Ark. What would make him go there? What made her think he was there? And how would he find the money? Nobody would ever find that money!

Daddy could—if he was on a tear!

She'd crossed the field. Now came the hard part. There was no path to the ark. First Mate stomped through the snow, kicking and clawing at drifts until they gave way. She knew twenty feet before the stairs that Daddy had been there—or he was *still* there. Telltale footprints marked a trail from the house to the stairs!

She didn't spy the cans of frozen manure until she drew nearer. Their imprints made harmless pockets in the snow. Daddy must have ducked when they came flying down. Why couldn't one of them have hit him on the head?

First Mate had never considered that if a winter got cold enough, even manure would freeze. Weather as cold as this wasn't in her vocabulary. This part of New Jersey was never so cold.

The gate to the deck was open. He'd kicked a path up the steps. She ran as fast as the cumbersome boots allowed.

At the top, she breathed a sigh of relief. The portal was closed tightly. Daddy had tried to kick it in, but Tad's padlocks held! Good ol' Tad. He sure knew how to put in a lock.

The secret was out, though. Daddy knew she kept money there. He'd be back, if not today, tomorrow. Maybe even in ten minutes. Maybe he was watching from behind a tree at that very moment.

First Mate ran to the rail and peered down. His tracks ran straight from the back of the house. There were no zigzags or turn-ins near any of the trees. Tate Bank was safe, but she had to move fast.

First Mate took the keys from around her neck and

opened the portal. The galley should have been dark, but it was bright. Then she saw it! The window—the porthole was smashed through!

The galley was a mess. She barely noticed, for another glare of light poured into her office. Oh no! He'd smashed open a bigger porthole!

Her stomach was a knot. Her heart screamed in agony. He was still here? There he was in the stateroom!

Her father didn't hear her, though. His back was to her. He knelt at the open pirate chest, pulling money out and stuffing it into his pockets.

The knot in her stomach turned to pure rage.

"How dare you?" she shouted.

Daddy turned around, startled.

"Put my money back!"

His eyes were crazy. He picked the packs of money he'd dropped and then the ledger, which lay near them.

"So how are you, Miss Loan Shark?"

He threw the book at her, but First Mate ducked. It fell harmlessly behind her.

"You missed!" she snapped.

"Too bad," he said. "My own daughter a loan shark . . . I don't have enough trouble with them, and you have to turn into one?

"You know," he continued, flipping the edge of a pack of bills, with his thumb, "if I'd had this, I could have broken the bank the other night."

"You would have lost it, like you lose everything," First Mate snapped back.

The words had popped out uninvited, but she was glad.

"Watch yourself," Daddy warned.

"You put my money back. It's not yours!"

"My daughter, the loan shark," Daddy repeated, stuffing more packs of ten-dollar bills into his pocket.

"At least I haven't delivered my soul to the great AC," she retorted.

"You're pushing it," Daddy warned.

"Pushing who? My father? He isn't around anymore. He left some goon who's working for a bigger goon in a boat yard."

Daddy was ready to break. First Mate knew it, and it scared her, but she couldn't help spitting out a few last words.

"Too bad Elizabeth isn't here. You could dangle her from the deck—or maybe Christopher. It doesn't matter. They're just your kids. Mom can have two more any old time."

"You're a damn thief!" Daddy shouted. "You think I didn't read your ledger?"

"I'm the only one in this family who has enough sense to care what happens to us! What do you think I'm doing here? Having fun? *No!* I'm trying to get the money together to buy back your business. That's what!"

She knew she ought to run, but she held her ground. So what could he do to her? Kill her? Good. Then he'd go to jail and maybe there'd be a chance for the kids.

Suddenly, her father burst into laughter. It was a wild

sound that bounced off the walls of the little room.

"Did you think that twenty-two thousand dollars was a good down payment? Do you know how much the land alone is worth? A couple of million—that's what. And you thought your penny-ante racket was really going to make a difference?"

Even a sapling bending with the wind has a snapping point. First Mate was no different. Her father's mocking words flashed before her eyes like lightning. She sprang at him. She punched. She scratched. She screamed. She bit. She kicked.

"I hate you! I hate you! You animal! You pig! You sleaze!"

She called him every name she'd ever heard on his docks. She called him names written in the cubicles of ladies rooms, names scrawled on walls, names she would be totally mortified to know she even knew—and she had no idea that she said a word. First Mate was totally out of her mind.

Her father didn't fight back. Instead, he crouched with his arms over his head. He was a man who worked with his hands. His body was hard, and she really didn't hurt it. But her hatred—*that* tortured him to the depths of his soul. He let his First Mate pummel and kick until she was exhausted. Then he took her in his arms and let her cry.

Perhaps it was the love of her grandparents, his parents, whose spirits stood nearby to warm them both. Perhaps it was the shock of seeing his eldest child fall to pieces. Perhaps it was an angel or two lending their holy light. Mr. Tate began to say again and again, "I'll never gamble. I promise. I'll get the help you asked me to get. I'm sorry, First Mate. I'm so sorry."

First Mate regained her senses. She knew that her head rested on her father's shoulder. She heard him talking to her, but she didn't listen. She didn't care anymore.

25

"If the words, 'I'm sorry' solved all problems, then the whole world would get on its knees and beg forgiveness for whatever. My father says he's sorry, but so what? I don't even care anymore. My mother says she's sorry, but I still hate her," First Mate told the strangers who sat with her around the table.

She was in the basement of a church somewhere in a town way north of Shadow Lawn. It wasn't even on the ocean.

Mom and she had driven up together. Mom was upstairs in the big meeting for the problem gamblers. First Mate had wanted to go to that one, but since she wasn't a compulsive gambler, she couldn't. The people in charge said she had to sit down here.

Actually, this meeting wasn't that bad. It was all kids. Some were older, some younger, but all of them had a father or a mother or both who couldn't stop gambling.

That's not quite right. Their parents did stop most of the time, but a boy named Carl was now saying that his father had just gambled away the rent money.

"My mother says he's out of here if he pulls it again. I think she means it this time."

"Whatever happens, it's not your fault. You didn't cause it and you can't cure it," said a boy who looked like he might be in fifth grade.

Some of these kids were young!

"I should have brought my little brother," First Mate whispered to the girl next to her.

She didn't reply. You're supposed to pay attention to the person talking, kind of like school, First Mate supposed, but no teacher.

After the meeting, Mom was crying so hard that they had to wait to drive home. First Mate was disgusted. She gave her a tissue and told her to blow her nose. She was so tired of her mother crying all the time. Well, at least Mom wasn't asking First Mate to take care of whatever made her cry.

Daddy was on tranquilizers—so who cared? At least he wasn't gambling. Actually, he was meeting with Charlie, trying to figure a way to buy the business back. What a mess!

The kids were at Angel's. She and Miss Sally were minding them.

So much had changed too quickly. Some of it stunk, like First Mate was told she couldn't boss the kids around anymore. Mom had to. It was her job. Bummer!

Then First Mate's counselor told her that her grams was wrong.

"She never should have told you to take care of things. You're just a child. It isn't your job."

"I'm almost thirteen!" First Mate retorted, indignantly.

"You need to worry about schoolwork, and boys, and what to wear to the next dance," the counselor replied.

Actually, First Mate wasn't going to school, not for a few days more. Mom and Daddy agreed that it would be better for her to stay at home. It wasn't her fault that her classmates were calling her the Loan Shark's Daughter.

Mom even went to school and told Miss Vail that First Mate had the flu. Then old Iron Nail told Mom a thing or ninety about First Mate!

"If I were an alcoholic, I'd at least be able to explain why I didn't know what was going on," Mom said when she got home.

She didn't cry, though. She just gave First Mate a year of assignments to finish. Daddy wouldn't let her out until she did them, not that she could go out anyway, since she was supposed to have the flu.

Angel came by and told First Mate that a lot of kids in school were upset about her being sick. Was she going to double their interest for next week's payment? First Mate told Angel to tell them that from then on, they didn't have to pay *any* interest. They did have to pay their loans, though, ten percent a week. That was a fair way to end Tate Bank.

She told Angel to collect the money and keep it in one of her father's vases. She still didn't trust her parents. The $23 thousand dollars *(not $22 thousand)* was in a new bank in accounts that only First Mate had to sign. Mom was researching a fund that would pay more interest than the bank offered.

"That will be your college," Mom told her.

Forget it, First Mate thought. She'd done a bit of research herself. If she waited long enough, she might really be able to buy that business, and put it in PJ's name —if he didn't turn into a gambler.

"Am I still the Loan Shark's Daughter?" First Mate asked Angel.

"Not really. Tad's spreading word around that before the McLeans skipped town, they'd rented the house to Charlie," said Angel.

"Did they?"

"Beats me. Tad swears that Charlie isn't a loan shark or anything bad. He just invests in businesses that will make him a lot of money. Tad's father investigated. Either way, don't worry. When I tell the kids they don't have to pay interest on their loans, you'll be a hero."

One Friday night, First Mate, Mom, PJ, and Daddy went back to that church in North Jersey. Miss Sally and Angel minded the rest of the kids.

First Mate and PJ were allowed to attend the big meeting, at least until they saw their father stand in front of everybody and say.

"My name is Pete, and I'm a compulsive gambler."